Dante moved across to her, making her gasp at his sudden closeness.

His strong hands took possession of Cami's thigh.

"Oh." She almost cried at the intensity of his touch, but the relief that came behind the pain had her shuddering and melting.

"That feels really good."

She gave herself up to it. Swirls of desire fluttered into her belly as his attentions went on. She tried not to reveal her reaction, even as secretive parts of her pulsed in yearning and her mind turned to thoughts she could no longer suppress.

His hands climbed her thigh again and she held her breath. What if he touched her *there*?

"Cami."

She barely heard him, his voice was so low.

"I don't want you to be embarrassed by the way you react to me."

"Look at who we are. It's so wrong." It was true, yet she was turned inside out by the stillness of his hands, aching with longing because he was so near and yet so far.

"It's not smart." His arms gathered her to sit across his lap. She was so weak, she floated into place, entranced by the glow of desire in his eyes. "But it's not wrong."

One Night With Consequences

When one night...leads to pregnancy!

When succumbing to a night of unbridled desire, it's impossible to think past the morning after!

But with the sheets barely settled, that little blue line appears on the pregnancy test, and it doesn't take long to realize that one night of white-hot passion has turned into a lifetime of consequences!

Only one question remains:

How do you tell a man you've just met that you're about to share more than just his bed?

Find out in:

Look for more One Night With Consequences stories coming soon!

Dani Collins

CONSEQUENCE OF HIS REVENGE

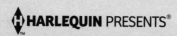 **HARLEQUIN** PRESENTS®

Recycling programs
for this product may
not exist in your area.

ISBN-13: 978-1-335-41925-5

Consequence of His Revenge

First North American publication 2018

Copyright © 2018 by Dani Collins

Printed in U.S.A.

Canadian **Dani Collins** knew in high school that she wanted to write romance for a living. Twenty-five years later, after marrying her high school sweetheart, having two kids with him, working at several generic office jobs and submitting countless manuscripts, she got The Call. Her first Harlequin novel won the Reviewers' Choice Award for Best First in Series from *RT Book Reviews*. She now works in her own office, writing romance.

Books by Dani Collins

Harlequin Presents

The Secret Beneath the Veil
Bought by Her Italian Boss
Vows of Revenge
Seduced into the Greek's World

The Sauveterre Siblings

Pursued by the Desert Prince
His Mistress with Two Secrets
Bound by the Millionaire's Ring
Prince's Son of Scandal

The Secret Billionaires

Xenakis's Convenient Bride

The Wrong Heirs

The Marriage He Must Keep
The Consequence He Must Claim

Seven Sexy Sins

The Sheikh's Sinful Seduction

Visit the Author Profile page
at Harlequin.com for more titles.

To all the dreamers among us:

I first conceived of this story when I heard the Olympics had been awarded to Whistler, British Columbia. That was at least two houses and three computers ago. At the time, becoming a published romance author was a dream that I wouldn't see fulfilled for years. Yet here is that story, in your hands.

Dreams don't always come true right away, but they do come true. Chase yours. You'll get there.
xo

CHAPTER ONE

"How could you fire me? I haven't even started work yet!"

Cameo Fagan tried to keep her voice to a hiss so it wouldn't echo across the hotel lobby, but she couldn't keep the panic out of her tone. She had already given up her job at the other hotel and, far worse, she had given up her *apartment*.

"Technically it's a withdrawal of the offer of employment," Karen hurried to say, holding out a splayed hand that begged for calm. She was the HR manager for the Tabor chain of boutique Canadian hotels. A mutual friend had put them in touch six months ago, when the renovations had been in full swing at this Whistler location. The Tabor was holding a soft opening on Monday with a gala for their official opening in two weeks.

Cami had thought she and Karen got on like a house on fire. She'd pretty much been hired on the spot.

"But…" She waved toward the narrow hall behind the front desk. It led to the offices and the very basic, but extremely affordable, staff quarters in the basement of the hotel. "I was going to move in this weekend."

Karen gave her a helpless look. She knew as well as Cami did that apartments in Whistler were impossible to find, especially on short notice. "It wasn't my decision. I'm really sorry."

"Whose was it? Because I don't understand." *Don't cry*, she willed herself. The universe did *not* have a plan to constantly pull the rug every time things started to go her way. She refused to think like that.

Even though it often felt exactly like that.

Karen glanced around the lobby where a handful of decorators were measuring and holding up swatches while workmen were putting the finishing touches on the fireplace mantel.

Lowering her voice even more, Karen said, "It hasn't been announced yet, but Tabor was bought out by an Italian firm. I guess the previous owners were in trouble after all of this." She lifted her gaze to the mural painted on the ceiling, one of many high-end touches included in the refurbishment.

That indication of deep pockets was why Cami had been willing to give up her very good job and take a chance here. Now her stomach clenched.

Italian? Or *Sicilian*?

"Are the new owners starting from scratch with the hiring? Because I'll interview again. I don't mind."

Karen's shoulders fell and she shifted uncomfortably. "It was, um, you he didn't want. Specifically."

"Me!" Cami's references were stellar, her work ethic highly praised. She went the extra mile every time. "He thinks I'm too young?" She'd run into that before, but when she explained how much experience she had, she was usually given a chance. It couldn't be sexism. Karen seemed to be keeping her management position.

"I'm really sorry." Karen looked and sounded sincere. "I don't understand it myself, but I submitted the list of hires and yours was the only name he scratched. He was quite adamant."

"Who?" Cami didn't want to believe she could still be haunted by the Gallos, but her heart was plummeting into her shoes. The universe didn't have it in for her. Nor did the Italians. One Sicilian seemed to, though.

The elevator pinged, cutting off whatever Karen was about to say. Her gaze slid to the opening doors. "Him," Karen said. "Dante Gallo."

Cami didn't have to ask which man Karen meant. Everyone in the group wore smart business attire, but one wore his bespoke suit with more assertiveness and style on a frame that was tall and alpha-postured. His jaw had a shadow of sculpted stubble and his dark hair was close-cropped, but devilish. His stern brows and sharp gaze stole any hint of approachability from his otherwise beautiful features. He was both gorgeous and severe. The kind of man used to getting his way by any means necessary, powerful and confident enough to make life-altering decisions in a blink. The women trailing him were flushed and sparkly-eyed, the men awestruck and quick-stepping, anxious to please.

Cami was awestruck herself, even feeling a coil of something in her abdomen that was sensual and wicked and *wrong*, especially when his predatory attention swiveled to her the way a hawk's head turned when a hare caught its attention.

Her heartbeat picked up as his focus honed in.

The entire planet stopped spinning as their gazes clashed. Or, rather, she felt as though they were caught in some kind of time slip. Everything continued to whirl around them in a whistling blur while thick amber soaked in, filling her veins with a honeyed sweetness that held them suspended in a muted world. Her vision dimmed at the edges, glowing golden. She stopped breathing. Something ancient resonated in her, a vibration as old as life itself.

That internal quiver expanded. Sensual warmth suffused her in a way that had never happened. She told herself this acute awareness of self and him was the heat of surprised recognition and anticipation of a confrontation. Animosity, not attraction. She had stalked him a couple of times online and had imagined a face-to-face conversation a million times. This was shock at finally having her opportunity, not fascination.

Definitely not desire pinching a betraying sting between her thighs.

She clawed back from her lack of self-control and found her resolve. This time, she wouldn't be leveled without a whimper of protest. Maybe he had a right to be angry with her father, but this grudge had gone on long enough. Did he really think he could destroy her just because of her name?

As her pulse beat a war drum in her ears, she waited for recognition to dawn in his features.

It didn't come, which was insult to injury. Her confidence began to waver while tendrils of vulnerability crept in.

Then she realized his gaze was heating with interest. *Male* interest. His forbidding mouth relaxed the way a man's did when a woman invited him to approach because attraction was reciprocated.

The sizzle under her skin became a conflagration, heating her all over, teaching her by fire that she was part of the human race after all. She did a lot of people-watching from behind her hospitality counters and was always intrigued by the way people coupled up. It baffled her because she had never felt such a simple and immediate pull herself. A receptiveness that couldn't be hidden.

Today, it happened. Basic animal magnetism took hold of her, shocking in its power because it was completely against her will. Mortifying, since she was the one providing the entertainment for Karen and anyone else who wanted to notice. She was sending all the wrong signals with her dumbfounded, dazzled stare, but her gaze was glued to his.

A slither of defenselessness went through her. She didn't want to react this way! Trolling online hadn't prepared her for the force of masculinity that came off him, though. He made her ultra-aware of her femininity. Her body made tiny adjustments, standing taller, stomach tightening. Her fingers itched to touch her hair.

The reaction was as disarming as he was, causing a fresh shyness to burn her cheeks.

Nerves, she insisted to herself. Pique. Genuine frustration at losing the job she had thought would finally give her the chance to get ahead. All because of him, she reminded herself, and used her animosity to grapple past her overwhelmed senses. And yes, maybe she owned some of the responsibility for his grudge, but *no*. She had tried really hard to fix things. Enough was enough.

She forced herself to step one foot in front of the other, advancing on the lion whose tail was flicking in lazy concentration. He looked entirely too powerful and ferocious. Too *hungry*. Each step brought her into a light and heat that threatened to sear her to her soul, but she ignored the adrenaline and excitement coursing through her arteries.

While he wore a hint of a smug smile because she was approaching him and not making him work for it.

"Mr. Gallo." Her voice seemed to fade as she spoke. She had to clear her throat. "Might I have a word?"

No one had spoken to him in such an imperative tone since he was a child. Dante bristled, but the reflexive assertion of superiority that rose to his lips didn't emerge.

Like most men, he categorized women very quickly into yes, no, or off-limits. Wedding ring? No. Coworker? Off-limits—for now.

Neatly packaged brunette with skin like fresh cream, a figure that didn't stop, and rose petal lips that managed to hold a curve of innocence and sin at the same time? One who moved with a dancer's grace and possessed the strength of character to look him in the eye without flinching?

"Yes" wasn't a strong enough word. She was a new category. Have to have. *Mine*.

That lightning-quick bite of hunger was disturbing. He had a healthy sex drive—*very* healthy—but one he easily controlled, always relegating it to non-work hours.

Yet with this woman his brain switched off, and his libido quickened in anticipation. Why? He searched for what made her different. Her clothes were low-end, but well-chosen to showcase her figure. Her breasts bounced a little, ample and firm, making him wonder about her bra. Lace? Demi-cup? Her round hips promised a nice plump ass atop those trim thighs, making the words, "Turn around," simmer in his throat.

The particular shade of plum of her blazer framed a thin, white line against her collarbone. A scar? A twist of protectiveness went through him. He had a strong impulse to brush back her rich, dark hair and kiss that spot. Make it better.

Embers of desire glowed hotter in his belly, thinking of the ways he would pet her and stroke her until neither of them knew anything but pleasure. Until they drowned in it. He liked the look of her wavy tresses. The spill of her hair moving as she walked. No hairspray. He could run his hands through that shiny fall, gather those silky strands in his fist as he held her still for a kiss that would appease and ignite...

Damn. He was going to tent his pants if he wasn't careful. She was only a woman. They weren't hard to come by. Never had been. He was here to work and indulge his grandmother, not take up with a local for after-hours fun. His entire world was one of responsibility and duty to his extended family. Selfishness was not an option. Hadn't been since his youthful foray into chasing a personal dream had exploded in his face, cracking the very foundation of his family's existence.

For the first time in a long time, however, he saw something he wanted strictly for himself. Not that he saw her as a thing—although he was barbarian enough to experience a certain titillation at the idea of owning a woman—but there was more. As she paused before him, potential hovered between them, too abstract to grasp, too real to ignore.

He forced his gaze to her face, trying to work out why her pretty, but not particularly striking features were impacting him so deeply. The women he usually went for were socialites. They wore layers of makeup that enhanced their features to the highest degree, and invited him with seductive smiles. They oozed sophistication and a desire to please.

This one was a natural beauty with lovely arched brows and a tipped-up nose. Her bare face made her look rather innocent while her eyes were a pedestrian hazel arranged in a starburst of brown within a circle of gray-green.

When had he ever looked so closely at anyone's eyes before?

When had he ever seen such a gamut of emotion? On her, they truly were windows to the soul. He read intimidation and bravery and something that made him think of butter and honey melting on his tongue.

He had an urge to laugh, not in dismissal, but enjoyment. So few people challenged or excited him these days.

"Let's go into my office." He waved at what would be the manager's office after he was satisfied this investment would turn a profit. His cousin, Arturo, was quite the vulture for deals like this, and usually handled the transition of a buyout. Once Arturo had heard their grandmother wished to tag along, however, his calendar had suffered a conflict.

Dante hadn't thought much of Arturo's priorities, but rather than scold him, he'd opted for taking the opportunity to spend a few days with the woman who had raised him—a woman he reluctantly acknowledged wasn't immortal.

She was supposed to be here soon, for a tour and lunch he recalled with distraction, glancing at the clock and feeling a pull of priorities. In this moment, this younger, nubile woman captured nearly all of his attention.

He closed the door. "I don't believe we've met." He held out his hand, palm itching for the feel of her in his grip. He might never let her go.

Her chin set and she took his hand in a firm, no-nonsense shake that was surprisingly powerful, sending a thrill rocketing through him. He wanted to tighten his grip and hang on. Pull her in and race to the inevitable.

When she spoke, he was too nearly lost in the clear, engaging tone of her voice to make sense of the words.

"I'm Cameo Fagan. Your new manager."

Her name ricocheted inside his skull, tearing holes in his psyche. All of his assumptions about her, where they might be going and how their association would progress, became a tattered mess. In the blink of an eye, ten years dissolved. He was watching his competitor announce a self-driving car that bore shocking resemblance to the one Dante was creating. All the money and time he had invested evaporated. The shock of the loss put the final stressor on his grandfather's heart, and it gave out.

Dante was left with an enormous hole in the family finances, extensive dependents looking to him to take up the charge and a bitterness of betrayal that sat on his tongue to this day.

He dropped his hand, so appalled with the way her soft heat left an imprint in his palm he brushed it against his thigh.

She flinched, and her erotic mouth trembled briefly before she firmed it, setting her chin a notch higher.

He waited for his sexual interest to fizzle. And waited. But the *No* that screamed through him was his inner animal, howling in protest at being denied. His libido *wanted* her. The rest of him recoiled in disgust. How could he be the least bit attracted to a *Fagan*?

"You're not to be on this property." He had made that clear after seeing her name on the list of new hires. One email to his office in Milan had confirmed she was related to *the* Stephen Fagan. That had been that. Her father had betrayed him. He wouldn't trust another one of them ever again.

He reached for the door latch, ready to expel her, distantly anticipating the physical struggle if it came to that.

She didn't move, only folded her arms, which plumped her breasts. "I don't know how they do things in Italy, but this is Canada. We have laws against wrongful dismissal."

He left the door closed, frustration morphing into fury. A desire to crush. He'd never met anyone who had lit his fuse as quickly or made it burn so hot. White and blistering. But he kept his tone icy cold.

"Italy has laws against theft. Most go to jail for it. Some, apparently, escape to Canada before they're convicted. Perhaps I should take *that* up with your government."

Her breath sucked in and her pulse throbbed rapidly in her throat. Her eyes were hot and bright. Tears? Ha.

"You're being paid back," she said through clenched teeth. "That can't happen if I don't have a job, can it?"

"Even if that were true, it wouldn't make sense for

me to give you money so you could give it back to me, would it? No gain in that for me."

"What do you mean, 'even if it were true'?" She dropped her fists to her sides.

"Let's pretend such a thing as compensation is even possible, since the design of my self-driving car had potential to earn indefinitely, but I've never seen a red cent from anyone, so—"

"Where has it been going, then?"

The sharpness of her tone sent a narrow sliver of doubt through him, thin as a fiber of glass, but sharp enough to sting because he almost fell for her outrage. He very nearly *wanted* to believe her, his body was that primed for her on a physical level.

But that was a Fagan for you. They could make you believe anything.

He shook off his moment of hesitation with a snap of his head. Trust led to treachery. He couldn't, *wouldn't*, trust her.

"Don't pretend your father has made any effort to compensate me. He hasn't. He *can't*."

That took her aback. Her complexion faded to gray, sending a brief shadow of concern through him.

"Of course he can't." Her brows pulled into a distressed knot. "He's dead."

She looked from one of his eyes to the other, expression twisted in confusion, as if she thought he ought to know that.

He didn't keep tabs on a man who had cost him a fortune and set his family back, leaving him at his most vulnerable. Dante was so furious at her temerity, at her attempt to work another con on him, and with himself for being momentarily drawn by her, he let one vicious word escape.

"Good."

It was far below him. He knew it even before her lips went white. Her mouth pulled at the corners as she tried to hold on to her composure, but those wide, far from plain Jane eyes of hers grew so dark and wounded, he couldn't look into them.

"You've done me a favor," she said with a creak in her voice. "I'd rather starve than work for someone who could say something like that."

She moved to open the door, but his hand was still on the latch. Her body heat mingled with his own, charging the air. The scent of fresh mountain air and wildflowers filled his brain, making him drunk.

"Let me out."

He saw the words form on her pink lips more than heard them. They rang in his head in a fading echo. He didn't want to. The encounter had become so intense, so fast, he was reeling, not sure if he'd won or lost. Either way, it didn't feel over.

Cold fingertips touched the back of his hand. Her elbow caught him in the ribs before she pushed down and pulled the door open, head ducked. Her body almost touched his. He thought he heard a sniff, then he was staring at her ass—which was even more spectacular than he'd imagined.

She escaped.

He slammed the door closed behind her, trying to

also slam the door on his impossible desire for her. On the entire scene.

There was no reason he should feel guilty. The wrong her father had done him had been malicious and far-reaching. Dante had foolishly dropped the charges in exchange for an admission of guilt and a promise of compensation, letting the man escape because, at the time, his life had been imploding. His grandfather's sudden death had meant Dante had to set aside his own pursuits and take over the complex family business. Its interests ran from vineyards to hotels to exports and shipping.

All of that had been put in jeopardy by the loss of the seed capital his grandfather had allowed him to risk on his self-driving car dream. The consequence of trusting wrongly had been a decade of struggle to find an even keel and come back to the top—yet another reason he wanted to give his grandmother some attention. He had neglected her while he worked to regain everything she and her husband had built.

Cami Fagan ought to be *grateful* all he had done was refuse to hire her.

Nevertheless, that broken expression of hers lingered in his mind's eye. Which annoyed him.

Someone knocked.

He snarled that he didn't want to be disturbed, then flicked the lock on the door.

Cami was shaking so hard, she could barely walk. She could barely *breathe*. Each pant came in as a hiss through her nose and released in a jagged choke.

Get away was the imperative screaming through her, but she could hardly see, she was so blinded by tears of grief and outrage. Good? *Good?* Had he really said that? What a bastard!

She was so wrapped up in her anguish, she almost missed the faint voice as she charged past an old woman sitting on a bench, half a block from the Tabor's entrance.

"Pi fauri."

Despite drowning in emotion, Cami stopped. She and her brother *always* stopped, whether it was a roadside accident or a panhandler needing a sandwich.

Swiping at her wet cheeks, she raked herself together. "Yes? What's wrong?"

"Ajutu, pi fauri."

Cami had a few words in a dozen languages, all the better to work with the sort of international clientele who visited destinations like Whistler. In her former life, she'd even spent time with Germans and Italians, picking up conversational words, not that she'd used much beyond the very basics in recent years.

Regardless, *help* was fairly universal, and the old woman's weakly raised hand was self-explanatory.

"I'm sorry, do you speak English? *Qu'est-ce que c'est*?" No, that was French and the woman sounded Italian, maybe? *"Che cos' è?"*

The woman rattled out some breathless mumbles, but Cami caught one word she thought she understood. *Malatu.* Sick. Ill.

She seated herself next to the woman, noting the

senior was pressing a hand to her chest, struggling to speak.

"I'm calling an ambulance. We'll get you to the hospital," Cami told her, quickly pulling out her mobile. *"Ambulanza. Ospedale."* One didn't race with champions down the Alps without hearing those words a few times.

She could have gone back into the Tabor and asked Karen to call, but she had her first-aid certificate, and this was exactly the type of thing she'd been doing since her first housekeeping position at a motel. The woman was conscious, if frightened and very pale. Cami took her pulse and tried to keep her calm as she relayed as much information as she could to the dispatcher. With the woman's permission, she was able to check her purse and provide the woman's name along with some medication she was taking.

"Do you have family traveling with you? Can I leave a message at your hotel?"

Bernadetta Ferrante pointed toward the Tabor, which sent a little shiver of premonition through Cami, but what were the chances? Dante Gallo seemed to be traveling with an entourage. Bernadetta could be related to anyone in there.

She asked a passerby to run into the hotel to find Bernadetta's companion, then pointed into the sky as she heard the siren. *"Ambulanza,"* she said again. "It will be here soon."

Bernadetta nodded and smiled weakly, fragile fingers curling around Cami's.

"What the hell have you done?" The male voice was so hard and fierce, it made both of them jump.

Cami briefly closed her eyes. *Of course it was him*. What were the chances of two head-on collisions in a row?

Bernadetta put up a hand, expression anxious.

Dante said, "*Non tu, Noni*," in a much gentler tone, before he returned to the gruff tone and said, "I'm speaking to her."

The ambulance arrived at that moment. Cami hovered long enough to ensure she wasn't needed to give a statement, then slipped away. Bernadetta was already looking better, eyes growing less distressed as she breathed more easily beneath an oxygen mask, while Dante left to fetch his car and follow to the hospital.

Cami trudged through the spitting spring rain to the next bus stop, only wanting distance from that infernal man. At least the crisis had pulled her out of her tailspin. Tears never fixed anything. She had learned that a long time ago. What she needed was a new plan. While she waited for the bus, she texted her brother.

My job fell through. Can I sleep on your couch?

CHAPTER TWO

MAKING COOKIES WAS the perfect antidote to a night of self-pity and a morning of moving boxes. Besides, she had a few staples to use up and a neighbor to thank.

When the knock sounded, she expected Sharma from down the hall. She opened her door with a friendly smile, cutting off her greeting at, "Hell—"

Because it wasn't Sharma. It was *him*.

Dante Gallo stood in her doorway like an avenging angel, his blue shirt dotted by the rain so it clung damply across his broad shoulders. He was all understated wealth and power, with what was probably real gold in his belt buckle. His tailored pants held a precision crease that broke over shiny shoes that had to be some custom-crafted Italian kind that were made from baby lambs or maybe actual babies.

Oh, she wanted to feel hatred and contempt toward him. Only that. She wanted to slam the door on him, but even as her simmering anger reignited, she faltered, caught in that magnetism he seemed to project. Prickling tension invaded her. Her nipples pinched, and that betraying heat rolled through her abdomen and spread through her inner thighs, tingling and racing.

Woman. Man. How did he make that visceral distinction so sharp and undeniable within her? Everything in her felt obvious and tight. Overwhelmed.

Claimed.

Hungry and needy and yearning.

She hated herself for it, was already suffering a kick of anguish even as his proprietary gaze skimmed down her, stripping what little she wore. The oven had heated up her tiny studio apartment to equatorial levels, so she had changed into a body-hugging tank and yoga shorts. Her abdomen tensed further under the lick of his gaze.

Stupidly, she looked for an answering thrust of need piercing his shell, but he seemed to feel nothing but contempt. It made that scan of his abrasive and painful, leaving her feeling obvious and callow. Defenseless and deeply disadvantaged.

Rejected, which left a burn of scorn from the back of her throat to the pit of her belly.

She should have slammed the door, but the timer went off, startling her. With emotion searing her veins, she made a flustered dive toward the oven and pulled out the last batch of cookies, leaving the tray on the stove top with a clatter.

Pulling off the mitt, she skimmed the heel of her hand across her brow. What was he even doing here? Yesterday's interaction had been painful enough. She didn't need him invading her private space, judging and disparaging.

She snapped the oven off and turned to see him shut the door as if she had invited him in. He stood behind the door, trapping her inside the horseshoe of her kitchenette.

Her heart began thudding even harder, not precisely in fear—which was frightening in itself. Excitement. How could part of her be thrilled to see him again? Forget the past. He was a cruel, callous person. *Good.* She hated him for that. Truly hated him.

She didn't ask how he'd got in the building. She wasn't the only one moving this weekend. The main door had been propped open the whole time she'd been loading boxes into Sharma's car and taking them to the small storage locker she'd rented.

This felt like an ambush nonetheless. What other awful thing had he said to her yesterday? She set aside her oven mitts and said, "You're not welcome on this property."

He dragged his gaze back from scanning her near empty apartment. His eyes looked deeply set and a little bruised, but she didn't imagine he'd lost sleep over *her*.

A weird tingle sizzled in her pelvis at the thought, though. She'd tossed and turned between fury and romantic fantasies, herself. He was ridiculously attractive, and this reaction of hers was so visceral. In her darkest hour, she hadn't been able to resist wondering, if they didn't hate each other, what would that look like?

Tangled sheets and damp skin, hot hands and fused mouths. Fused bodies? What would *that* feel like?

Not now. Definitely not *him.*

She folded her arms, hideously aware she only had a thin shelf bra in this top, and her breasts felt swollen and hard. Prickly. If she had had a bedroom, she would have shot into it and thrown on more clothes. Her chest was a little too well-endowed to get away with something so skimpy anywhere but alone in her apartment, especially when her nipples were standing up with arousal.

She became hyperaware of how little she wore. How close he stood and how small her space was. The studio apartment ought to feel bigger, stripped to its bare bones—a convertible sofa that had been here when she moved in, along with an oval coffee table, a standing lamp and a battered computer desk. All that remained of her own possessions was an open backpack and the sleeping bag she was taking to her brother's. The emptied space felt airless and hollow, yet bursting with tension. Like her.

"What are you doing here?" she asked when he didn't respond to her remark.

"My grandmother would like to thank you."

Could he say it with more disdain?

"Is she…" She took in the signs of a rough night, suddenly gripped by worry. "I called the hospital. They don't share much if you're not family, but said she'd been released. I thought that meant she was recovered."

"She's fine."

"Good." She relaxed slightly. "What happened?"

"Asthma. She hasn't had an attack in years so didn't bring her inhaler."

There was definitely something wrong with Cami because even though he took a tone that suggested speaking to her was beneath him, his accent and the subtle affection and concern in his tone made his talk of asthma and an inhaler sound ridiculously kind and endearing. Sexy.

The heat of the oven was cooking her brain.

"Well, I'm glad she's all right. I didn't realize she was your grandmother—"

"Didn't you?"

What now? Her brain screeched like a needle scraping vinyl. It struck her that a tiny part of her had wondered if he was here to apologize. Or thank her himself. Wow. How incredibly deluded of her.

It made her ridiculous reaction to him all the more unbearable. Of all the things she hated about him, the way he kept making her feel such self-contempt was the worst. She normally liked herself, but he made her mistrust herself at an integral level. He said these awful things to her and she still felt drawn. It was deeply unnerving. Painful.

"No," she pronounced in a voice jagged by her turmoil. "I didn't. And yes, before you ask." She held up a hand. "I would have helped her even if I'd known she was related to you. I don't assume people are guilty by association and treat them like garbage for it."

She had to avert her gaze as that came out of her mouth, never quite sure if she could truly claim her father was innocent. He had signed an admission of guilt, that much she knew, but had told her brother he was innocent. If he *was* guilty, was it *her* fault he'd stolen Dante's proprietary work and sold it to a competitor? She just didn't know. The not knowing tortured her every single day.

It made her uncertain right now, one bare foot folding over the other, when she wanted to sound confident as she stood her ground. Her culpability was reflected in her voice as she asked, "How could I know she was related to you? You don't even have the same last name."

"Sicilian women keep their names." He frowned as though that was something everyone should know, then shrugged off her question. "I'm not on social media much, but she is. It wouldn't take more than a single search of my name to pull up our connection."

"It would take a desire to do so, and why would I want to?"

"You tell me. Why did your father target me in the first place? Money? Jealousy? Opportunity? You knew who I was yesterday. You must have looked me up at some point."

Further guilt snaked through her belly. Had she been intrigued by him even then? Not that she had admitted to herself, but how could she not want to know more about a man who had such power over her and remained so out of reach?

"Maybe I did." She tried a shrug and a negligent shake of her head, but only managed to loosen her ponytail. She grabbed at it, dragging his gaze to her breasts, raking her composure down another notch. Challenging him was a mistake. It was an exercise in bashing herself against bulletproof glass with no hope of reaching whatever was inside. She knew that from the few times she had been desperate enough to try getting in touch, to plead her case, only to be shut out.

At least she was in a better place these days, even though it was still a precarious one. Her brother was looking after himself now, if barely scraping by under student loans. Her being jobless and homeless didn't mean he would be without food and shelter, as well. She actually had a place to go to now that her own life had imploded again.

That meant she didn't have anything left to lose in standing up to Dante. She dropped her arms and lifted her chin.

"Are you accusing me of somehow causing your grandmother's asthma so I could call for treatment?"

"No. But I think you recognized her and took advantage of an opportunity."

"To do what? Be kind? Yes. Guilty!"

"To get on my good side."

"You have one?"

He didn't move, but his granite stillness was its own threat, one that made a dangerous heat coil through her middle and sent her pulse racing.

"You haven't seen my bad one. Yet." Then, in a surprisingly devastating move, he added, "Cami."

She felt hammered to the floor then, all of her reverberating with the impact of his saying her name.

A flash in his eyes told her he knew exactly how she was reacting, which made it all the more humiliating.

Sharma chose that moment to knock, forcing her to collect her bearings. Cami had to brush by him, which caused him to move farther into her apartment. Her whole body tingled with awareness, mind distracted by thoughts of his gaze touching her few things, casting aspersions over them. Why did she even care how little he thought of her?

"Hi," Sharma said with a big smile.

Cami had actually forgotten between one moment and the next who she was expecting. Her own baffled, "Hi," reflected how out of sorts she was, making Sharma give her a look of amused curiosity.

"Everything okay? Oh, you have company." Intrigue lit her gaze, and she waved at Dante. "Hi. Are you our new neighbor?"

Cami caught back a choke. The Dante Gallos of the world didn't live in places like this. He'd probably wipe his feet on the way *out*.

"He's just visiting." Flustered, she set a brown bag of cookies on a small box of dishes she wasn't keeping, but that Sharma's young family might find useful, and returned Sharma's keys at the same time. "Thanks for the car today."

"It was bad enough you were moving out of the building. You can't leave *town*," Sharma said, making a sad face as she accepted the box. "What happened with the job?"

"I'll explain later." Cami waved a hand to gloss past the question, not willing to get into it with the demigod of wrath looming behind her, skewering her so hard with his bronze laser vision she felt it like a pin in her back. She was a butterfly, squirming under his concentrated study, caught and dying for nothing because her plain brown wings wouldn't even hold his attention for long.

Sharma's gaze slid over to him and back as if she knew Dante had something to do with it. "Okay, well, nice to meet you." She waved at Dante, then said to Cami, "Gotta run to get Milly, but say goodbye before you leave."

"I will."

As she closed the door, Cami ran through all the should-have-saids she'd conjured last night, as she had replayed her interchange with Dante in his office. Through it all, she had wished she could go back and change a decade's worth of history, all to no avail.

No matter what threats he was making, however, she knew this was a chance to salvage something. To appeal to whatever reasonable side he might possess. Maybe. Or not. Perhaps talking to him would make matters worse.

Still, she had to make him see she was trying to make amends and hopefully ease this grudge he had. It was killing her on every level; it really was.

As Dante waited out Cami Fagan's chat with her neighbor, his brain was still clattering with all the train cars that had derailed and piled up, one after another, starting with the news her father was dead—which had been strangely jarring.

Initially, before their association had gone so very wrong, he'd looked on Stephen Fagan as a sort of mentor. Dante's grandfather had been a devoted surrogate after Dante's father died, and an excellent businessman willing to bet on his grandson, but he hadn't had the passion for electronics that Dante possessed.

He'd found that in Stephen, which was why he had trusted him so implicitly and felt so betrayed by his crime. Maybe he'd even believed, in the back of his mind, that one day he would have an explanation from the man he'd thought of as a friend. Damaging as the financial loss had been, the real cost had been his faith in his own judgment. How had he been so blind? Something in him had always longed for a chance to hear Stephen's side of it, to understand why he would do something so cold when Dante had thought they were friends.

Hearing Stephen was dead had been… Well, it hadn't been good, despite his claim otherwise. It had been painful, stirring up the other more devastating loss he'd suffered back then. All the losses that had come at once.

As he'd been processing that he would never get answers from Stephen, someone had knocked insistently, informing him his grandmother was unwell. Rushing outside, what had he found?

Cami.

In the confusion, she'd slipped away, but she'd stayed on his mind all the while his grandmother was treated. The moment she had recovered, his grandmother became adamant that she thank the young woman who had helped her.

Back when she'd been grieving the loss of her husband, Dante hadn't dared make things worse by revealing how he'd put the family's security in jeopardy. It was one of the reasons he hadn't pressed charges against Stephen—to keep his grandmother and the rest of the family from knowing the extent of their financial woes. He hadn't wanted anyone worrying more than they already were.

Instead, with the help of his cousin, he'd worked like a slave to bring them back from the brink.

That silence meant Noni didn't understand why he was so skeptical of Cami's altruism. He didn't want to tell her he would rather wring Cami's neck than buy her a meal, but he wasn't about to let his grandmother go hunting all over town for her good Samaritan, possibly collapsing again. He also sure as hell wasn't going to give Cami a chance to be alone with his grandmother again. Who knew what damage would be done this time?

So, after a restless night and a day of putting it off, he'd looked up her address from her CV and had come here. He'd walked up the stairs in this very dated building, wondering what sort of debts her father had paid off since he clearly hadn't left much for his daughter, and knocked.

Then *Smash!* She had opened the door, plunging him into a blur of pale pink top that scooped low enough to reveal the upper swells of her breasts and thin enough her nipples pressed enticingly against it.

Her red shorts were outright criminal, emphasizing her firm thighs and painting over her mound in a way that made his palm itch to cup there. The bright color stopped mere inches below that, covering the top end of a thin white scar that scored down past her knee.

He'd barely processed the old injury when she whirled away in response to a buzzer. The fabric of her shorts held a tight grip on her ass as she turned and bent to retrieve something from the oven, making his mouth water and his libido rush to readiness.

He had spent the night mentally flagellating himself for being attracted to her at all, let alone so intensely. Cami was beyond off-limits. She was a hard *No*. Whatever he thought he might have seen in the first seconds of their meeting had been calculated on her part. Had to have been.

She had known who he was.

And now he knew who she was, so how could he be physically attracted to someone who should repel him? It was untenable.

Yet the stir in his groin refused to abate.

She turned from closing the front door, and her wholesome prettiness was an affront. A lie. He curled his fist and tried not to react when she crossed her arms *again*, plumping that ample bosom of hers in a most alluring way. Deliberately?

"I don't know how to convince you that I had no ulterior motive yesterday, but I didn't." Her lips remained slightly parted, as though she wanted to say more but was waiting to see how he reacted first.

"You can't. She wants you to come to the hotel

anyway. To thank you. Not the Tabor. The one where we're staying."

Surprise flickered across her face, then wariness. "And you're here to intimidate me all over again? Tell me not to go anywhere near her?"

"I'm here to drive you." Was she intimidated? She wasn't acting like it. "But it's true I don't want you near her. That's why I'll supervise."

"Ha. Fun as *that* sounds—" She cut herself off with a choked laugh. Her ironic smile invited him to join in the joke, then faded when he didn't.

Something like hurt might have moved behind her eyes, but she disguised it with a sweep of her lashes, leaving him frustrated that he couldn't read her as easily as he wanted to.

She moved into the kitchen to transfer the last batch of cookies onto the cooling rack. "Too bad you didn't put it off until Monday. I would have been gone. Tell her I've left town."

He moved to stand on the other side of the breakfast bar, watching her.

Such a domestic act, baking cookies. This didn't fit at all with the image he'd built in his mind of her family living high off his hard work and innovation. Nothing about her fit into the boxes he'd drawn for Fagans and women, potential hires or people who dined with his family. Nothing except…

"Unlike you, I don't lie, especially to people I care about."

"Boy, you love to get your little digs in, don't you? When did I lie to you?"

When she'd mentioned he was being paid back, for starters, but, "Forget it. I'm not here to rehash the past. I've moved on." Begrudgingly and with a dark rage still livid within him.

"Really," she scoffed in a voice that held a husk. Was it naturally there? An emotional reaction to his accusation? Or put there to entice him? "Is that why you fired me without even giving me a chance? Is that why you said it was 'good' that my father is dead? My mother died in the same crash. Do you want to tell me how happy you are to hear *that* news?" The same emotive crack as yesterday charged her tone now, and her eyes gleamed with old agony.

He wanted to write her off as melodramatic, make some kind of sharp comeback so she wouldn't think she could get away with dressing him down, but his chest tightened. Whatever else had happened, losing one's parents was a blow. He couldn't dismiss that so pitilessly.

"I shouldn't have said that," he allowed, finding his gaze dropping to the scar etched onto her collarbone. She had that longer one on her leg, too. Had she been in the accident? He tried to recall what he had known about Stephen Fagan's family, but came up with a vague recollection of a wife and a forgotten number of children.

Why did he find the idea of her being injured so disturbing? Everything about this woman put him on uneven ground. He hated it. There was already a large dose of humiliation attached to her father's betrayal. He'd been soaked in grief over losing his grandfather, but guilt, as well. The old man had loved him. Indulged him. And Dante had failed so very badly, even contributing to his grandfather's death with his mistake.

An acrid lump of self-blame still burned black and hot within him. He had had to take that smoldering coal in hand, shape and harden it with an implacable grip, and pull himself into the future upon it.

Since then, nothing happened without his will or permission. He was ruled by sound judgment, not his libido or his temper. Certainly not his personal desires. Yet anger had got the better of him yesterday. *She* had. And emotion was threatening to take him over again today, especially when she muttered, "No. You shouldn't have."

The utter gall of her was mind-blowing.

She clattered the cookie sheet and spatula into the sink. Her ponytail was coming loose, allowing strands of rich mink and subtle caramel with tiny streaks of ash to fall around her face. It gave her a delicate air that he had to consciously remind himself was a mirage. That vestige of grief in her expression might be real, but the flicker of helplessness was not. Fagans landed on their feet.

"Look," he said, more on edge than he liked. "Helping my grandmother was a nice gesture, but I'm not giving you back that job, if that's what you were after."

She lifted her head. "It was a coincidence!" She dropped some cookies into a brown paper bag and offered it to him. "Here. Tell her I'm glad she's feeling better." Her hand tremored.

He ignored the offering. "She wants you to come for dinner."

"I have plans." A blatant lie. She set the bag on the counter between them.

"I'm not letting you hold this over me. Or skirt around me. Put on a dress and let's get it over with."

"I've packed all my dresses."

"Is that your way of asking me to buy you a new one?" He had played that game a *lot* and couldn't decide if it grated that she was trying it. Under the right circumstances, he enjoyed spoiling a woman. Cami's heart-shaped ass in a narrow skirt with a slit that showed off her legs—

"No," she said flatly, yanking him back from a fantasy that shouldn't even be happening. A pang of something seemed to torture her brow. Insulted? Please.

"What do you want, then? Because clearly you're holding out for something." He *had* to remember that.

"And you're clearly paranoid. Actually, you know what I want?" Her hand slapped the edge of the sink. "I want you to admit you've been receiving my payments."

"What payments?"

"Are you that rich you don't even *notice*?" She shoved out of the kitchen and whisked by him to the rickety looking desk, then pulled up short as she started to open a drawer. She slammed it shut again.

"I forgot. It's not here. His name is, like, Bernardo something. It's Italian."

"What is?"

"The letter! The one that proves I've been paying you back." She frowned with distraction, biting at her bottom lip in a way that drew his thoughts to doing the same. "My brother has the file, though. He took it last fall."

"Convenient."

"God, you're arrogant."

He shrugged, having heard that before. Recovering his belief in himself had been the hardest part of all. His ego had taken a direct hit after misjudging her father. He'd questioned himself, his instincts and his intelligence, which almost crippled him as he faced the Herculean task of recovery. In the end, he had no choice but to trust his gut above anyone else and get on with the work. He would have been dead in the water otherwise.

He refused to go back to self-doubts. He faced everything head-on and dealt with it as expediently as possible. "Let's get past the games. I know you have a hidden agenda. Speak frankly."

"I don't! I'm exactly what I look like. I applied for a job for which I am fully qualified. You came along with your sword of retaliation and cut me off at the knees. Then I was nice to a little old lady who happens to be your grandmother. Now I have to move and get back on my feet. *Again*."

Her hand flung out with exasperation as she spoke. She smelled like the cinnamon and vanilla she'd been baking with, sweet and homespun. All smoke and mirrors.

"How was I supposed to know you would buy the Tabor when I interviewed six months ago? I'm not trying to pull a fast one on you. You're the one out to get *me*." She managed to sound quite persecuted.

He shook his head, amazed. "You look like you're telling the truth, but so did your father. It's quite a family talent, I have to say." Then, because he was so damned tempted to reach out and touch her, he neutralized that secret weapon of hers. He gave her luscious figure a scathing once-over and said, "Of course, he didn't work the additional diversions you employ."

Her jaw dropped open with affront, but her gaze took a skitter around the room. She blushed, seeming disconcerted. Caught out, even. "I'm not— You showed up here unannounced! As if I'd throw myself at *you*."

"No?" He was needling her, determined to maintain the upper hand, but that tiny word seemed to flick a switch.

She flung back her hair to glare at him. "You're the last man on earth I'd want anything to do with!"

She faltered as she said it and tried to give him a scathing once-over, but her lashes quivered. He could tell by the way they moved that her gaze traversed his torso and down to the muscles in his abdomen. His stomach tightened with the rest of him. In those charged seconds, he grew so hot, his clothes should have incinerated off his body.

When she brought her gaze back in a flash of defiance, there was a glow of speculation in their depths. The light shifted, or, more accurately, the fog of animosity in her eyes dissolved into a mist of desire.

The air shimmered, hot and oppressive between them. All an act, he reminded himself, but, *What the hell*. He ought to get *something*.

"If you want to talk about compensation, I'm listening." He suddenly seemed really close. His voice was like whiskey-soaked velvet.

"What?" She took a step back, reeling from the way her body was betraying her. She was trying to rebuff him, but everything about him overwhelmed her senses.

She came up against the wall and he flattened his hands on either side of her head, not touching her, but caging her. She set her hands on his chest, alarmed then intrigued by the layers of heat and strength that pressed into her fingertips. He was pure vitality, enticing her hands to splay and move in a small stroke of curiosity that quickly edged toward greed.

How did he disarm her so quickly? How had they even wound up like this? She could feel his sharp nipples stabbing into the heels of her palms and it pleased her. Excited her. She wanted to run her hands over his chest and onto his lower back, exploring everywhere.

She had to quell a whimper of helplessness. This desire was terrifying and exhilarating at once. Deadly, yet impossible to ignore.

His pupils swallowed all the color in his eyes, drawing her into the darkest unknown.

"What are you offering?" His arousal was so tangible in his voice, it felt like a caress from her shoulder down her chest. A sweep of bumps rose on her skin and her breasts grew heavy and swollen.

"Cold?" The corners of his mouth deepened and she couldn't read his eyes.

This was bizarre and damning, yet compelling. She felt as though a drug had been released in her system that made her languid and euphoric. She didn't move away. Couldn't. Her breaths moved unevenly, and she could swear she felt the brush of his erection against her.

His muscles were like iron. Rather than shoving him away, she dug her fingers into flesh that had no give, exploring against her own willpower. How could the inherent strength in him, that wasn't even being exerted against her, make her so weak?

He was doing something to her, though. It was a force that gripped her without effort. He wasn't even touching her. She was the one touching him, yet she couldn't escape. Couldn't make her body push him away. She stood there and watched his face draw closer, filling her vision. She waited, lips parting, mind blank, until his mouth touched hers. *Hot*.

Why she held still for his kiss, she didn't know. It was beyond stupid, yet she let it happen, wanting to know something she couldn't even define. She tensed, maybe expecting punishment. Cruelty, even. He wasn't a kind man. She already knew that.

He *was* cruel as he kissed her, but in a way she couldn't have anticipated. He used gentleness to tease her lips into opening wide, then slowly worked their mouths into a firmer fit, angling and sinking closer, waiting until she was moving her mouth against his before he settled in to fully plunder.

A deep quiver rang through her. Recognition. As though she'd been waiting all her life for this. Her body gave a small shudder and sighed in relief. *This one*.

That should have scared the hell out of her, but she was so entranced by the sense of discovery, by the flood of heat and need, she let the kiss continue. She let it draw out, going on and on while she sank deeper and deeper into sweet pleasure.

She had never progressed much further than a kiss. Had never wanted to. Not like this. This kiss was beyond anything she'd ever known. It was *right*. It picked up all the pieces of herself she'd left scattered and broken and fit them together again, making her feel whole and alive. Omnipotent.

Worldly and womanly and exalted.

Her fingers moved, testing the firmness of his pecs, then slid in a blatant caress across the flex of his muscles, squeezing and shaping, tracing the ridges of his ribs and flowing to the hollow of his spine.

He growled and dropped his hands to her waist, stroked her hips in a sweeping circle of his big hands, then he cruised his palms up to cup her breasts, thumbs raking across her nipples. The twin sensation was so sharp and electric, she bucked.

He settled the weight of his hips against hers, pinning her to the wall, forcing her to take that continued gentle torture of her nipples. Heat plunged into her loins, and there was no denying what she felt there. She was screamingly aware of the stiffness of his arousal against her. His thighs were hard and hot, pressing hers to open so her mound was firmly in contact with that hard, hard shape. She throbbed under the pressure of him against her so intimately. When had she ever wanted something so earthy and base? Never. Not before this moment and this man who kissed her to the point she stopped thinking.

His thumbs circled and teased with an expertise that made her wriggle, the acute stimulation lifting her hips into his. *More.* That's all she could think as she kept kissing him, suffocating, but unwilling to stop. *Keep doing that. I want more.*

The way they were consuming each other was blatant and more primal than anything she'd ever known. Her arms lifted to circle behind his neck, arching her breasts into his relentless hands. He pinched her nipples and she whimpered at the pleasure-pain, legs growing weak and pliant under the pressure of his. She stroked her fingers through his hair, luxuriating in the feel of the short, crispy strands, before drawing his head down to increase the pressure of his kiss to the point of near pain. It wasn't enough. It could never be enough.

His tongue thrust in and her hips ground against his, seeking the most acute sensations she could find. Nothing had ever made her act so animalistic. That's why she'd never gone all the way. She'd never been compelled to by her own body, but oh, the way he was massaging her breasts was driving her crazy. She was so aroused, she actually mewled with loss when he lifted his head and dragged his hands down to her hips.

He watched her as he held her still for the blatant, deliberate thrust of his hard sex against hers. The flush on his face was barbaric, dark and satisfied as she gasped and met his erotic movement with a wanton, inviting rock of her own. A moan escaped her lips as she climbed ever higher on the steps of arousal toward the precipice of bliss.

Her hands clenched in his shirt and she pressed her head into the wall, giving up her lower half to his, inhibition gone. She had to bite her lip against groaning even louder as he rubbed against the bundle of nerves that was barely protected by the thin fabric of her yoga shorts. Her eyes fluttered closed and she held her breath, quivering with tension, so close—

With a hiss, his hands hardened on her hip bones before he thrust her back into the wall, releasing her to step away.

Stunned, she scrambled for purchase on the empty wall, panting as she fought to remain standing. Her body *screamed* for his, making this rejection the height of cruelty.

His cheek ticked, but he didn't look nearly as shattered as she felt. He was aroused, but held a cynical gleam in his eye that cut her to the bone.

"We'll finish talking about that later. Get dressed. Comb your hair. We're running late."

"What?" Her knees threatened to buckle.

If she thought he sounded strained, or as though he balanced on a razor's edge of his own, the impression evaporated as he smiled, merciless and self-assured. The peaks and valleys in his face stood out in sharp relief, light and dark. Beautiful and indifferent.

"Since the compensation you're offering comes with such a high rate of interest—" the corner of his mouth curled at his own pun "—I'll give you a chance to make your case. But my grandmother is expecting us." He glanced at the gold watch on his wrist, the face black and numberless, with only two needle arms. "We need to leave."

"I'm not going anywhere with you."

"You want to finish talking now?" His withering inflection told her they wouldn't be using their mouths for words.

CHAPTER THREE

"No!" CAMI SHOVED off the wall and stumbled toward the sofa, where her backpack sat open. She grabbed at the cowl-necked pullover that came to hand and hugged it to her front. "Get out."

She wanted him away from her so she could make sense of what had just happened.

His nostrils twitched and he gave her a long moment to absorb that by leaving, he was getting what he wanted. He wasn't obeying.

"I'll wait in my rental. If you're not out in ten minutes, I'm coming back."

Her heart pounded. She bit her lip against saying another word, gripped by incredulity, but having enough sense to know she needed him out of here so she could get herself back under control. As the door clicked, she sank onto the sofa and tried to decide if she wanted to cry or scream or swear. Maybe all of the above.

Why had she kissed him? Let alone so lustfully he thought she was offering to prostitute herself? It was humiliating!

It hadn't felt humiliating while they were doing

it, though. He'd made her feel things she'd never felt with anyone.

Why *him*?

All her life she'd waited for the right man. Dating and relationships were distractions she couldn't afford, so avoiding going all the way hadn't been difficult. It wasn't as though she thought of her virginity as holy or golden, but she came with baggage and liabilities. She didn't feel like a catch. When she did have sex, she expected it to be with someone who had earned her trust, loved her for who she was and deserved this part of her life that was, as yet, unmarred by memories of anyone else.

Now Dante Gallo had barged in and set the bar on sexual encounters to unimaginable levels. She very much feared reaching it again would be unattainable. Where would she meet another man who made her feel like that?

"Oh!" She buried her face in her pullover, still restless and tingling. *Aroused*, damn him. She was sensitized and filled with yearning. She would have slept with him. Totally would have let it happen, which wasn't her *at all*. She'd never understood when other women behaved wildly, having sex with courier drivers in the back of a van or going home with a stranger, saying things like, *I was really into it. We got carried away.*

Cami had disparaged such stories. *She* never got carried away. She had secretly feared there was something wrong with her. Like she was a tiny bit frigid.

Nope. She just hadn't meant Dante Gallo.

But he was the *wrong* man. Totally, utterly and completely.

Yet she could still feel that deliberate way he had thrust against her. In that moment, she had felt as carried away and *with* someone as it was possible to feel. She had thought they were both in the moment, edging toward ecstasy together.

A fresh rush of excitement flooded her loins along with a sting of fresh mortification. He hadn't been nearly as caught up, and she should have been thinking about—

She jerked her head up, ardor finally subsiding as she remembered what they'd been talking about before the kiss.

How did he not know about her payments? She was so faithful about making them. Had been for five hard years, no matter what other financial disaster had befallen her. There was always something. A rent increase or her brother's new shoes.

Despite making a decent salary and living very frugally, she was consistently flat broke because she made the equivalent of a generous mortgage payment to Dante Gallo every single month.

His playing dumb about that had her popping onto her feet and dragging on some proper clothes. She didn't care about dinner with his grandmother, but she wasn't about to face him in next to nothing again.

Or let him come barging in after her.

She put on the outfit she had left out for her travel to Vancouver tomorrow. It was a classic wool miniskirt in charcoal, black tights and the soft blue pullover she had squeezed a couple of tears into a minute ago. A pair of knee-high boots that were actually worth a fortune finished it off. The mother of a ski student had given them to her because they hadn't fit in her suitcase back to France. That was precisely the reason Cami had left them out to wear tomorrow.

She felt tough and feminine and confident every time she zipped the supple leather up her inner calf. They had just enough heel to give her some swagger and always earned her compliments, boosting her ego.

She had needed that kick of self-assurance as she prepared to leave for Vancouver and her brother's decrepit sofa in his shared basement suite in a dodgy part of the city.

With a glance at the clock, she saw she had two minutes to run a brush through her hair and lock her door. She tapped her bank code into her phone as she walked outside, searching her recent transactions until she found the one from last month.

She glanced up as she reached the parking lot and paused.

Dante was on his phone, too, leaning on a black SUV. The rain had stopped, but the clouds were low and heavy, bringing on early dusk, casting him in uneven light. He was shadows and power and had touched her as if she belonged to him. She still felt his hands on her, still felt under his spell.

No. She was a steady, levelheaded, smart woman who controlled her own life. She had grown up fast and shouldered responsibilities way beyond her years.

Yet he erased that by lifting his glance. A fair

distance separated them, but she felt him take her in from eyelashes to boot tip.

She had never felt so anxious for approval. So green and uncertain in herself or her own autonomy. Her near climax at the touch of his body was right there, torturing her with her own weakness.

Yet, maybe there was a twisted piece of her that felt so guilty about her father, she wanted Dante's punishment and blame. Maybe that's why this attraction was blindsiding her this way.

"You look nice. *Grazij.*"

His words stung through her, mostly because she was so affected by the lukewarm compliment. "I didn't dress for *you*. Here." She strode forward, holding out her phone as if it was a shield that could deflect all his barbs and ability to undermine. "See?"

He didn't take the phone. He steadied her hand and glanced at the screen.

She held her breath, pulse tripping while she tried not to be affected by something so innocuous as his touch over the backs of her fingers. Everything they'd done in her apartment came rushing back to torment her. She wanted to pull back, but made herself stand there, heart hammering, watching for some kind of change in his expression. She thought she might have stopped breathing and begun to shake.

Dante didn't know what the hell he was looking at. He was still half-blind with lust. This woman had got him so hot, so fast, he'd nearly lost control from a randy bit of necking. She had gone from wary and surprised, to participating, to what appeared to be a surrender of the most exquisite kind.

Appeared.

Somehow, at the last second, he had remembered who she was and hadn't let her get the better of him. He'd had to stand out here in the spit of spring rain, counting down the minutes with a barely acknowledged hope that she would defy him. Speculating what he would do if she forced him to go back in there and finish what they'd started had *not* helped cool him off.

She had emerged on time, looking lovely in an elfin way, with her short skirt and sleeves falling past her wrist. Her hair was loose and lifted on the evening breeze while she closed in on him with purpose, her insanely sexy boots making soft splashes as she strode through shallow puddles in the pavement.

As she stood here with her hand trembling in his, he wondered how he'd found the will to leave her without stripping them both naked and driving into her. Was this closeness of hers still part of her act? He couldn't afford to think her reaction to him was anything but a put-on, but damn did he want to.

"Well?" An underlying huskiness in her tone seemed to stroke over his skin, making his back prickle.

"Well what?" He let a finger steal beneath the edge of her soft sleeve.

She snatched her hand back. "Do you recognize the amount?"

"No."

"It's the same every month. Who does your book-keeping?"

"My accountant." Why was she going on about this? "But I know where my money comes from and where it goes." He opened the door of the SUV.

"But—"

"Do you need help getting in? It's starting to rain again." The fat drops were falling in a more steady patter, soaking through his shirt.

She let out a huff of impatience and swung into the vehicle with surprising grace.

"Ask him," she demanded when Dante climbed behind the wheel. "Ask your accountant."

"She," he corrected, then rested his forearm on the steering wheel as he gave her a frustrated study. Was she really trying to prove something here? Or was it more of her shell game tactics? Either way, there was an easy fix. "Fine. Give me that." He held out a hand for her phone.

She tucked it into her chest. "What are you going to do?"

"Take a screen shot and send it to myself. I'll forward it to my accountant." He glanced at his watch. "But it's two in the morning there. She'll be asleep."

With a disgruntled scowl, she warily handed over her phone.

He turned the scratched fossil this way and that, giving her a side-eyed frown. "Is this what they call a 'classic'?"

"Do you know what they want for a 'free'—" she hooked her fingers into air quotes "—upgrade? Do not get me started on the racket that is cell phone plans."

He smirked, bemused by her ire against something so inconsequential.

He clicked the screenshot and tapped in his details. The whoosh sounded and a ping emanated from his pocket. He handed back her phone and took out his own, sent the message, then tucked his phone back into his chest pocket to start the engine.

"Oh, I wasn't—"

Her hand went to the door latch, but he was already backing out of his spot. The seat belt reminder pinged and rain drummed harder against the roof. He flicked the wipers to their highest setting so they *slap, slap, slapped.*

She gave a dismayed sigh and put on her seat belt. "I wasn't going to go with you."

"Why not?"

"Because an inch turns into a mile with you."

He considered that as he turned onto the main road. He didn't take anything from a woman that she wasn't willing to give.

"You didn't call a halt," he reminded. "I did."

A loaded silence filled the interior. Everything else might be an act, but she'd looked as close to finding fulfillment as he had. It made her too damned tempting.

"You'll be nice to my grandmother."

"I *am* nice, not that you would even know what that looks like. For instance, when I come across someone who needs help, *I help them.*"

"I'll withhold judgment on that." Fagans were self-interested, greedy, faithless and deceptive.

She waited until they were almost at his hotel to respond shakily, "You realize that my father stole your schematics and research. *I* didn't."

He slowed to turn into the entrance of the hotel, then braked beneath the colonnade and jammed the vehicle into park before he swiveled to confront her.

"You still benefited."

What might have been a wince of guilt dented her features, but the hotel's valet opened her door and she turned away to step out of the vehicle.

Dante slammed out of his side and strode around to hand over his keys, then led her through the lobby to the elevators.

"Where—?"

He waved her through the doors that opened, waiting until they closed to explain, "Some of my employees are staying here. I can't be seen dining with you."

"Oh, but you can be seen taking me to your room? Employees here know me. Maybe I don't want them thinking I'm some kind of escort. Did you think of that?"

"No," he replied without apology, and was now distracted by the idea of hiring her for an evening. Of having the power to order her to do *exactly* as he pleased.

As if she was imagining it herself, and had her own erotic images painting through her mind, a delicious pink blush rose along her cheekbones. Her lips parted to allow a sip of air, leaving her mouth looking incredibly inviting.

The elevator stopped, throwing her off balance.

He caught her elbow to steady her. "Really," he said, hearing how she affected him in the way his voice deepened to a graveled tone. "Your acting belongs on the screen."

Cami jerked out of his hold and escaped through the opening doors, then halted to glare back at him. It was really hard to stalk away in a huff when she didn't know where she was going.

He smirked. "Noni's room is this way."

He didn't take her arm again, but her skin tingled. All of her felt as if it floated, yet the anchor of his mistrust dragged at her. She didn't know how to prove herself to him, and was growing increasingly frustrated by the effort. If she didn't have this lack of defense around him, it wouldn't hurt so much, but it did.

"You won't bring up your father. She doesn't know anything about that." The sudden grimness in his tone sent a shiver through her.

As if she enjoyed talking about that. Her throat ached, but she didn't know what to say. She couldn't believe she was even here, going through with this dinner, but she *was* nice and didn't want to be rude to his grandmother just because Dante was clawing up her insides.

He paused to knock on a pair of double doors. A female butler let them in, mentioning that their hostess was taking a call and would join them in a moment. She offered to pour drinks.

Hovering with tension, Cami glanced around the suite. The drapes were closed, but she could tell it was one of the hotel's best, with a mountain view from the picture window. If she recalled correctly, there was a Juliet balcony outside the French doors. The gas fireplace was glowing, and a small dining table was set with china, silver, crystal and fresh flowers.

She had only ever been on the service side of places like this. She had to fight the urge to strike up friendly conversation with the butler, whom she regarded as her equal, rather than try to find common ground with Mr. Tall, Dark and Daunting.

He was watching her as though he expected a misstep any second.

Just as she thought she would incinerate from the eye contact, Bernadetta appeared, coming through from the bedroom with a warm smile. She was small and plump, gray hair smoothly gathered in a round bun. Her color was much better, the lines in her face softened. She immediately apologized for not using her English yesterday.

"You were distraught. I'm so glad you've recovered," Cami said, accepting the woman's gentle touch on her shoulders and soft kisses on each of her cheeks. She smelled like rosewater and motherly love, melting Cami's heart if not her tension.

Bernadetta greeted Dante with similar affection.

"Thank you for fetching her. You're a good boy." She patted his cheek, which seemed a ridiculously tender thing to do to a man who was so obviously a *man*.

Bernadetta took the armchair, forcing Cami to lower onto the love seat next to Dante, thighs almost touching.

"I'm blessed with a doting family," Bernadetta said. "That's why I was delayed greeting you. I've been taking calls all day. That was Arturo, Dante's cousin. He's in Australia, looking at a property, but he saw my post in the family group and wanted to reassure himself I was feeling better. He seemed to think your name sounded familiar," she said, taking Cami by surprise. "Do you know him?"

Startled, she shook her head. "I don't know any Arturos, no."

The wrinkles in Bernadetta's forehead deepened with puzzlement. "He asked me if Cami was short for Cameo."

"It is, but I don't believe we've met. Unless... I did live in Italy briefly, ten years ago. I was only fourteen and it was Northern Italy. The Alps. Not Sicily."

Dante's expression had hardened.

She licked her lips. She wasn't the one steering this conversation into dangerous waters! "If I met him in passing, I don't recall," she mumbled in a rush.

Bernadetta leaned forward with interest. "What brought you to Italy?"

"Skiing." Her conscience pressed like a bed of nails on either side of her as she said it, now a victim of her own censure, not just Dante's. "My parents moved us there so I could train under a world-class coach." One who had cost a fortune.

She looked to the hands she had folded in her lap.

Was her dream the reason her father had stolen from Dante? She would never know. But she would always feel it was a factor, one that made her responsible for all that had happened to Dante, her parents and her brother. If her father hadn't wanted to give her that training, he wouldn't have stolen the money. They wouldn't have had to leave Italy and come back to Canada. They wouldn't have been on that icy road outside Calgary that had cost her parents their lives.

"Downhill? You were racing for Canada?"

"And slalom. I was hoping to make the team, but—" She cleared her throat. It took all her effort to smile through the excruciating pain of losing so much. Her chance, her coach, then her parents. For a while, she'd even lost her brother. She had learned how to slap a glossy prevarication on harsh realities, though. "I was injured and couldn't continue."

"You don't ski at all anymore? That's a shame."

"Oh, I do," Cami said ruefully. "It's a bit of an addiction, but I can't do it full-time, otherwise I'd give lessons for a living. I offer private lessons to children when I can. It works out well for tourist families. Parents can enjoy the more challenging runs knowing their children aren't getting lost or winding up on a run beyond their level."

"What a lovely thing to do. There, Dante. Let me send you skiing with Cami, as a thank you to both of you for looking after me so well on this trip."

Her pulse spiked. *Oh, heck, no.* "Dinner is more than enough," she hurried to protest. "Honestly."

"Pssh. Dante works too hard. You'll be doing me another favor. I was going to ask him to take me up the gondola tomorrow, to force him to take a break, but after my mishap, I'm just as happy to stay indoors."

"I wouldn't want to impose on your family time." She glanced at Dante, unable to read his stony expression. "I'll be leaving for Vancouver soon, anyway." *Help me out here.*

"Oh, when is that? My niece and her husband will be coming to fetch me Monday, to drive me into the city. I'm staying with them until I fly back to Sicily. We have more than enough room to take you with us."

Dear Lord. Could she dig herself any deeper? Cami silently begged Dante to conjure an excuse on her behalf.

He only sipped his drink and said, "Thank you, Noni. I didn't think I'd have the chance to ski, but I'd like that." The cool, half-lidded look he sent Cami warned against rejecting the old woman's offer.

Spend the day with him? What sort of sadist was he?

And what sort of masochist was she that she held out a shred of hope for…something if she did. Softening? Understanding? A chance to redeem herself in his eyes?

"That's very generous of you," she mumbled into her own glass, confused by her reaction. "Thank you."

The first course arrived, and the butler invited

them to the table. Cami was able to keep the conversation with Bernadetta to neutral topics from there on, but it was a difficult evening. An oppressive yearning made her hyperaware of Dante and her own body language. Of the fact she was supposed to ski with him tomorrow.

Mix her one true love with a man she hated? She *had* to get out of it.

"That was weird that your cousin thought he knew my name."

Dante had worried the whole thing was coming out of the bag and grudgingly appreciated the way Cami had changed the subject.

"He does." Dante glanced at the phone that had been pulsing regularly through dinner. Arturo wanted to hear from him. "Our mothers were the eldest of seven sisters. We ran wild on the estate all summer, especially after I lost my parents and lived with my grandparents permanently. He didn't share my passion for cars or electronics, but he always encouraged me to follow my aspirations."

For a time, Dante had wondered if it was an attempt to push him from being their grandfather's successor, but Arturo had never enjoyed taking responsibility. He'd matured enough to be an asset on the acquisitions side of the family business, identifying opportunities like the Tabor, but back in their youth he'd been a playboy, partying and gambling in the stock market. He'd done surprisingly well at it, fortunately.

"When our grandfather died, Arturo was with me through every step, especially helpful with the way I'd been compromised by your father. He offered more than moral support. Financing. I needed it." It was a lowering thing to admit, one that made his teeth clench to this day. "We're like brothers. Naturally, he wants to know why I'm consorting with the family that betrayed me."

Color rose in her cheeks.

The elevator stopped and the doors opened.

"I can find my own way home," Cami told him as she crossed the lobby in a brisk clip.

He paced her easily, not even bothering to acknowledge the remark, only handing his ticket to the valet as they reached the entrance.

"We'll wait in here where it's warm." Cami hadn't brought a coat, and the spring weather was looking closer to winter now that night had fallen.

"What if you're seen with me?" Cami challenged in a scathing whisper, giving him a wide-eyed look that was equal parts impending doom and disdain.

Dante's thoughts on fraternization were evolving, given their kiss, but he would address that after he'd had time to work through it more thoroughly.

That's why he hadn't yet returned his cousin's texts. He should be pushing Cami out the door and out of his life, but he couldn't forget—literally couldn't stop thinking about—the way she had felt in his arms. All through dinner, while she'd been advising his grandmother on which shops carried the best local art, he'd been thinking about taking her to his room.

Spending the night with her, finishing what they'd started in her apartment.

Sleeping with his enemy would be the height of insanity, but there could be something very satisfying in it. As long as he maintained the upper hand. Carnal hunger gnawed at him, warring with his good sense.

The valet arrived, and they walked outside where the chill on the damp air made their breath fog. She waited until Dante had pulled away from the hotel to say, "I can't go tomorrow. I sold my skis, and I'm not letting your grandmother rent any for me."

His grandmother wasn't exactly on a fixed income, but, "I intend to pay."

"Then I am definitely not going."

"She'll want to see photos proving how much fun we're having." He enjoyed making that facetious statement, especially when it provoked a tiny noise of frustration in her throat. He smiled in the dark. "Why did you sell your skis?"

"Is that a real question? I don't have a job or a place to live." She spoke like she was explaining it to a child. "I needed cash to rent a storage locker."

He made the turn toward her neighborhood, which was in the most modest part of a very affluent resort town. "What did your father do with all the money?"

"You tell me," she said tightly. "You said earlier that I benefited from his crime, but I didn't. Not in any way that I can tell."

"No?"

She moved restlessly in her seat, muttering reluctantly, "Maybe I was supposed to. Maybe he was trying to pay for my training. I don't know. I was fourteen, totally in my own world, barely aware what a mechanical engineer *was*, let alone who he worked for or what you were making together. I was close to getting a sponsorship, not a huge one, but enough to help. It fell through. Maybe he got desperate."

Her tone of self-recrimination sounded real enough to niggle at him when he wanted to think of her as remorseless. "Did he have other debts?"

"Not that I know of. Living in Italy was expensive, I know that. We sold everything to go and had nothing when we came back. Both of my parents worked professional jobs, but we could only afford a tiny apartment in Calgary. They had a lot of hushed conversations, not saying much about any of it directly, but money issues were obvious. The only way I was able to train again was by getting my own job and saving up. After they were gone, and I knew more about what had happened, I assumed Dad had made a settlement of some kind. Gave the money back. That's why I was surprised so much was still owed."

"He promised to repay me every euro."

"I know." She clipped and unclipped the clasp on her handbag. "I've seen the statement he signed."

Any time over the years that Dante had looked at that document, he became so sick with himself, he walked away. Now he was finally confronting the past with a woman who beguiled even as she threatened a second betrayal. He ought to be running far and fast. Instead, he was thinking the unthinkable.

"The only thing Mom ever said about any of it was that he admitted to something he didn't do so he could come with us back to Canada and avoid a long legal battle."

What else would the wife of a criminal say to their children? "What about your brother? Older? Younger? Does he have money?"

"No." She snorted. "He's at university in Vancouver, trying to get into the medical program."

"He wants to be a doctor?"

"Yes."

"That's expensive. Postsecondary isn't covered in Canada, is it?"

"He has a couple of scholarships, but yes. He'll be up to his eyeballs in student loans for years by the time he's done, so there's been no benefit for him, either."

"I can check that, you know."

"Don't you dare even think of interfering with his plans," she warned with a tremble in her voice. "That's a red line for me. It really is."

And she would do what? He parked outside her building, finding her threats laughable. Useful. Clearly her brother was a pressure point.

She left the vehicle at the same time he did, and colored when she saw him come around to her side.

"You're supposed to wait for me to open it for you," he chided.

"This isn't a date. Why on earth would you walk me in?" On the heels of that, she made a noise of realization, turning her head to the side, profile flinching. The streetlamp above her showed the light rain condensing on her hair in tiny sparkles, highlighting skin that was alabaster smooth. Her expression showed a brief struggle. He heard her swallow before she spoke in a voice that held a pang. "I'm not going to kiss you again."

"No?" His chest tightened, and he made himself hold the distance that his libido was screaming at him to close. "Run inside, then."

She turned only her head to look at him, face shadowed. Angry? Maddened, certainly.

So was he. This shouldn't be happening. He ought to hate her. He did resent her. He resented this. But when she only stood there, blinking rapidly, he stepped forward and wove his fingers into her hair, clasping her head in his hands.

A helpless noise broke from her throat. More surrender than protest. She tilted her head back and parted her lips, offering her mouth to his. A gratified groan rumbled in his chest as he took the kiss she offered. Took and took and took, rubbing his lips across and against, parting and seeking and ravaging.

If he was being too rough, she didn't let on that she didn't like it. Her hands bunched into his shirt beneath his jacket, scratching lightly at his rib cage then clinging, pulling him in while her mouth moved under his and she moaned with pleasure that echoed his. When he swept his tongue into her mouth, she swirled her own against it, sucking delicately, making his hands tighten in her hair, driving him insane.

He was going to ache all damned night from this.

Everything in him wanted to take her inside and *take* her. But he remained standing there in the growing fall of rain, plundering the sweetness of her mouth until she finally pulled away to gasp for breath.

His own chest rose and fell like he'd been running a four-minute mile.

She dropped her hands and backed away another step, forcing him to let his own hands drop.

"Why is this happening?" Her whispered question sounded disturbingly vulnerable, like they were victims of the same tragedy, aligning them when he needed to remember she was only trying to coax him into forgiving her father's crime.

He was damned close to doing it, if she would only, "Ask me to come in." His voice wasn't anything he recognized, ragged with sexual hunger and hard with the imperative gripping him.

She shook her head. "No."

Toying with him?

She had the back of her hand pressed to her mouth. If her lips felt anything like his, they were hot and stinging. There was only one way to soothe that. His gut tightened in anticipation while he gritted his teeth in frustration.

He could accept that a trick of hormones had him reacting to a woman who was his mortal enemy. What he would not allow was for her to use his desire to manipulate him.

"Be ready early, then." He managed to speak as if his interest had already waned.

Her gaze came up, shiny in the silvery light. Wounded?

"I'm not skiing with you! The only thing I want to hear from you tomorrow is that your accountant has confirmed I've been paying you back all this time. Feel free to text an apology at that point."

"You just never quit, do you?"

"It's the *truth*."

"Be ready," he warned. "Or I'll make inquiries about your brother."

Her head jerked like it was a blow she hadn't expected. Like she didn't understand he would find every advantage and use it without mercy.

"My father called you a visionary, you know." She sounded disillusioned. "I remember because I was jealous that he talked about you with so much admiration. He was just as proud of me, but it still made me work harder, wanting to measure up to someone he regarded so highly. I thought you were someone worthy of his respect. I guess I was mistaken."

"As was I, thinking he was worthy of mine."

She sucked in a breath, proving he'd landed a jab as sharp as hers had been. He smiled despite experiencing no satisfaction.

"Good night, Cami."

"Good*bye*, Dante." She hurried away, sexy boots leaping over puddles, graceful as a gazelle.

As he watched her retreat, skin so tight he could barely breathe, he acknowledged that he was rooting for her. He wanted, by some miracle, to hear that she had been trying to make some sort of restitution to him. It would make this lust so much more palatable.

Which was why he was so disappointed when the email came through in the morning, proving yet again that Fagans were liars.

CHAPTER FOUR

"I DON'T UNDERSTAND." It was the understatement of the year. Of the decade. She couldn't even comprehend what she was seeing. Her stomach had plummeted into her shoes along with her heart, her blood and her brain. Even her breaths felt like she had to draw them with great effort from the center of the earth.

She looked from Dante's phone, to his remote expression, back to his phone. It still didn't make sense.

"How can there be no record?"

He released a very quiet sigh. "You've taken this as far as it can go, Cami. It's time to abandon this pretense of yours." His gaze was flinty with warning. Dislike?

Her insides grew sharp and jagged. A sick feeling churned in the pit of her belly.

"It's not a pretense!" It was a terrifying disaster.

Her heart picked itself up and began to run. Her mind whirled, trying to grasp at a course of action, but it was like trying to catch a snowflake, each one melting and disappearing on contact. This simply couldn't be true. He was wrong. His accountant hadn't looked hard enough.

"I need to talk to my bank," she managed weakly, touching her temple and finding it clammy. Surely they would have a sensible explanation. Please, God.

"It's Sunday."

"I can't wait to sort this out. It's thousands of dollars missing!"

"Is that right?"

"Don't be sarcastic!" It came out sharpened by the tears she was suppressing.

She had actually gone to sleep with a certain peace of mind, thinking she would finally be vindicated in his eyes. He would realize she wasn't the lowest form of life, and maybe they could move forward from there, toward…she didn't know what. Something she refused to imagine until it was possible, but it was beyond out of reach now. He still reviled her and, she suspected, thought even less of her for "lying" to him.

How could the money not be showing up in his account?

She had to tell Reeve. He had taken all the files last summer, when he'd been trying to get his student financing in place, to demonstrate need. They'd had a spat about it, actually. She hated anyone to know about their situation, feeling ashamed of it. He was incredibly bitter they were in this position at all—that *she* was. He couldn't help her pay it down. He needed every spare cent for tuition and food. He kept saying they had paid enough, but she saw no other option.

She texted him with shaky hands, keeping it vague,

just asking him to scan the most important documents, not saying anything about Dante's accountant.

She wasn't surprised when there was no response. Reeve often spent Sunday at the library or some other quiet location, catching up on assignments or reading.

When she lowered her phone, Dante lifted his brows in expectation.

"What? Oh, for heaven's sake! You can't expect me to go skiing." She was having a crisis over here. And he *hated* her. He couldn't possibly want to spend the day with her. She certainly couldn't withstand hours of his derision.

"I don't want to disappoint my grandmother."

She opened her mouth, wanting to claim a need to visit the bank but then remembering it wasn't open. She considered phoning the hotline, but doubted the after-hours customer service would be able to do anything. This felt like an in-person problem that would require an official ordering a proper investigation into her own records and the bank's.

"I'm catching a bus in a couple of hours."

"My grandmother invited you to travel with her to Vancouver tomorrow."

"And where do you suggest I spend the night? I'm turning in my keys on my way out of here." Her backpack was buttoned up, and she was wearing the same clothes she'd worn last night.

Dante lifted one corner of his mouth, as sexy as he was arrogant.

"With you?" Wicked temptation coiled through her, much to her chagrin. He knew it, too, which made it worse. "Please," she dismissed in a scoff she wasn't able to pull off. "I was not fishing for an invitation."

His brows twitched in a silent, *Sure you weren't.* "How much do you want?"

"To spend the night with you?" she nearly screeched.

"To play tour guide on the mountain," he drawled, not bothering to hide the amusement crinkling his eyes. Those tiny lines were annoyingly attractive, making her wish she could prompt a smile that attractive without the mockery at her expense.

Awful man, twisting her up like this. "A thousand dollars," she blurted.

"Done."

"I was joking!"

"I wasn't. Let's go." He jerked his head at the door.

"No."

"You want to negotiate spending the night, as well?" His tone lowered to a velvety, lusty tenor that wrapped her in erotic bonds.

"Stop treating me like I can be bought." Her voice was barely audible, not nearly as belligerent as she was going for. She was damned near pleading for him to show some mercy—which was futile.

His gaze dropped to the boots she was wearing.

She shifted her weight, unable to hide them. "These were a gift."

"Ah." *So supercilious.* "What sort of gift would you expect from me, then?"

"Respect?" she suggested sweetly.

He held his eyelids at a cool half-mast. "That's something you earn."

"And I would earn buckets by taking your money, wouldn't I? As I told your grandmother last night, I teach kids to ski. One of their mothers gave me these. They weren't from some random man I slept with. I don't do that."

His expression didn't change. He said nothing, not even a skeptical, *No?*

She blushed, all too aware of how off the scale her reaction to him was and how it sent all the wrong messages. Maybe he had a reason to wonder about her, considering the way she'd behaved with him, but— Oh, damn him anyway.

"Can you get out of my life, please?" She swept the hair off her brow, aware she was trembling. Teary.

How could he not be getting her money?

He pushed his keys into his pocket with a quiet jangle, gaze so intense it just made her feel all the more fragile. It was a struggle to keep her lips steady.

"I want to believe you, Cami, I really do," he said quietly. "But you can understand why I don't. Can't you?"

Her eyes grew hotter. "Can *you* understand that I'm freaking out, right now? I thought I was paying you back!" Her phone ought to be snapping in two. It was certainly going to leave a bruise across her palm where she was clutching it with all her strength.

His jaw hardened, and she heard a subtle exhale of tested patience.

Her phone rang. She glanced at the screen, saw it was Reeve. "Hi," she answered.

"What do you need those papers for? I thought you were on your way here."

"I haven't left yet." She flicked a glance at Dante, certain he could hear her brother as clearly as she could.

"Good, because Seth's brother just got here. I said you were coming, but if he could use the couch to-night—"

"That's fine." Cami tried not to wince. The suite belonged to Seth, so she couldn't really take the sofa from his brother. "I can stay with Sharma." Probably. "But can you send the scans? I don't want to wait."

"I'm at the library. It'll be a few hours before I'm home. Why? What's up?"

"I want to check something at the bank in the morning," she prevaricated, then hurried to forestall more questions. "I'll text when I'm on my way. Happy studying. Eat a vegetable. Coffee beans don't count."

"If you were a science major, like me, you'd know different. Over 'n' out."

She ended the call and texted Sharma, then faced Dante again. Why was he even still giving her the time of day?

Oh, she had such a burning desire to prove herself to him. If she could just get him to believe this one thing… But what would it change? Her father's be-trayal still existed. Nothing could erase that, and it left her so exhausted inside, she wanted to cry.

"*Now* are you ready?" He moved to shoulder her backpack.

"You really insist on skiing?"

"I do."

Was she rationalizing? Finding a reason to spend the day with him?

She was filling her day with the one thing guaranteed to work out her stress. That's what she told herself as she closed her apartment for the last time and followed him out.

Cami certainly knew her way around the village, the hill and, most important, skis. He bought some, since he would be in town a few weeks.

She quizzed him thoroughly about his preferences and experience before recommending a pair, shrugging off her extensive knowledge of edges and bounce, wax and seasonal conditions in the area. "I'm a geek for this, what can I say?"

She disappeared while he was picking out ski pants and a pullover, leaving him mulling that she had nothing to gain from what she had just done except personal enjoyment. There was no attempt to earn a commission or his favor. It seemed an act of selflessness, which aligned with her acting so kindly toward his grandmother, but still went against his preconceived assumptions.

The way she had seemed genuinely alarmed over the missing money transfer was another puzzle piece that didn't fit. He was trying to work out what she thought she could gain from such an outrageous lie when he met up with her at the lift line.

She wore rented skis and clothes he'd seen her pull out of her backpack, which she'd stored in the back of his SUV—a thin black turtleneck, skintight yoga pants and a lightweight red windbreaker. Sexy as hell.

His brain blanked, unable to think of anything else.

It didn't help that in that moment the sun broke through the thin film of clouds, making her that much more incandescent with silvery streaks in her hair. She perched a pair of sunglasses on her nose and smiled with an excitement that was contagious and utterly entrancing.

"You said you like powder?"

It was why he'd wanted an early start. All that rain in the village last night was reputed to produce a foot of talcum-like snow at the top. Left to his own devices, he might have found a pocket or two, but Cami knew all the bowls and untracked slopes and the shortest distance between them.

He let her lead, and they roared down one untouched run after another. By the time the snow was growing heavy under the warmth of afternoon sun, he was pleasantly tired.

"Lunch?" It was closer to happy hour.

"I should take a break," she agreed. "I haven't skied that hard in ages."

He frowned, realizing fine trembles were quivering through her. "You should have said you were getting tired."

"Your grandmother wanted us to have fun," she reminded. "I'll take the beginner run to the lodge. You can take the diamond, if you like."

"I'll stay with you, but there's a chalet midway, isn't there? Let's eat there."

She nodded, and he followed at a distance so he could make sure she didn't fall.

He'd watched her more than once today, convinced that at least her family's reasons for going to Italy had been genuine. She wasn't afraid of speed, and her turns were a thing of beauty, precise even now, when she was being lazy, playfully kicking up a spray of snow as she crisscrossed the slope.

She moved gingerly once they removed their skis and were shown to an outdoor table on the overlook, though.

Dante ordered white wine and shareable appetizers, then asked, "Have you pulled something?"

"Just an old break that wants to be babied." She buried the response in her glass of water, gaze hidden behind her sunglasses. Then her nose turned to the stark white peaks jabbing at the intense blue sky. "That would make a nice backdrop for a selfie if you want one for your grandmother."

He took out his phone and they moved to the rail. The view of rolling peaks gave a sense of being on top of the world.

They turned their backs to it and he flicked to his camera setting, looping his free arm around her. She stiffened and flashed a startled glance up at him, flushing with instant awareness.

The simmer of lust hadn't abated in him. Her slender figure was undeniably feminine, yet strong and resilient. She smelled like wilderness and woman.

The weight of her resting against him had his skin feeling too small to contain him.

As they held eye contact, and the pink in her cheeks deepened, the smolder inside him grew to an inferno, but there was more beneath the physical response. He was oddly pleased by this perfect day. Something like gratitude welled in him that she'd made it so enjoyable. He leaned in to kiss her, unable to resist.

She gasped and her mouth parted under his, receptive and delicious, clinging and encouraging, her hunger as depthless and instant as his own. As with the other two times, the match caught immediately. Passion flared so high and quick, it singed his brows.

With a tiny sob, she abruptly pulled her head back, lashes wet and blinking. "Please don't."

His blood drummed in his ears as he hovered inches from kissing her again, taking in the pang of her voice, nearly fearful, and the anguish in her wet lashes.

"I don't know how to handle this," she whispered. "Please don't embarrass me in front of people just to prove you can."

She wasn't playing coy. Her distress was real and worked like a burr into his heart, prickly and uncomfortable. He did like knowing he provoked such an unfettered response in her, but he wasn't trying to degrade her with it. He wanted to drown in it. *With* her.

She tried to slip away and he tightened his arm, snapping back to the business at hand. "Smile," he said gruffly, hand not quite steady as he held up his phone.

She swallowed, lifted her sunglasses into her hair and swept a fingertip under each eye, then tilted her face up to the screen. "Turn it to video."

He did and she smiled, fresh-faced and beaming with natural beauty, yet so unguarded, it caused an unsteadiness in his chest.

"Thank you, Bernadetta. We've had a wonderful day." Her voice was husky, and she blew a kiss with a hand that trembled.

"*Grazij*, Noni," he said, arm tightening around Cami in an impulse to protect and reassure. He wanted to insist he would never hurt her, but he already had.

The fist clenched with righteousness inside him gave a twist of guilt. He kept his turmoil from his expression as he scanned to capture the view behind them before ending the recording.

"*Grazij*, Cami," he said as he released her to send the clip.

"I enjoyed it." She flashed him a look of lingering vulnerability, then moved to their table, seeming to deliberately look for a more neutral conversation as she commented, "It's nice that you're so close to her. My grandparents were gone before I was old enough to remember them."

Their wine had been delivered. They sat, clinked, sipped and sighed.

"It's too bad she isn't seeing more of the area." Her sunglasses were still on her hair, leaving her serene, sun-kissed expression wide open for his admiration. She looked across the view the way he looked across the vineyard at home. Like it brought her peace. Restored her.

For one second, he wondered if he could blame Stephen for indulging her, if mountaintops were where she belonged. He shook off the damaging thought, saying, "She was here with my grandfather years ago. Nostalgia brought her. I think she's disappointed by the signs of progress. She prefers to stay in her hotel room where she can pretend he just popped out for ice."

The signs of age in her were eating at him.

"They traveled extensively when my grandfather was building their fortune. When she heard we'd bought property here and said she'd like to see it, I thought it was a resurgence of her old travel bug, but it's more about revisiting a place she enjoyed with my grandfather. That's why she walked to the Tabor the other day. I arranged a car, but she preferred memory lane. Last night at dinner was the first time she's talked about anything but being here with him. I don't mind. She's telling me stories I've never heard, but it's made me realize how much she misses him."

It made him realize how much he'd been in his own world, concentrating on work at the expense of spending time with her.

"How long were they married?"

"Almost fifty years."

"Amazing." Her gaze eased into wistfulness that

faded to melancholy. "It must have been so hard for her to lose him."

"It was."

"You must have been very close to him, too. You said you lived with them after your parents died? How old were you?"

"Eight." He scratched his cheek, becoming aware he was sharing far more than he meant to. He took a sip of wine.

"So young." She frowned, introspective. "But there's no good age, is there?" The empathy in her gaze dropped the bottom out of his heart. How had they come to get so personal? "Do you have brothers and sisters?"

"No." He had to clear his throat. The abandonment instilled by his parents' death had been unbearable, making him wish for siblings at the time, but it was a very long time ago. His grandfather's loss had hit him hard, though, stirring up his sense of being adrift. Losing his grandmother would be the same grief all over again, which was why he couldn't bear to contemplate it.

"But I have, quite literally, hundreds of cousins. Aunts and uncles galore." All of whom he was responsible for. If the weight of that was heavy at times, well, that didn't matter. They were all the family he had.

"I always thought being part of a big Italian family would be fabulous." Her mouth tilted. "Is it?"

"Sicilian," he was compelled to correct, then shrugged, impatient to move on from talking about himself. "I have no complaints. You have just the one brother?"

"Reeve, yes."

"Older?"

"Four years younger."

Their food came, a sampler of local specialties including elk tartar, seared scallops on nasturtium leaves and smoked salmon with sunchoke chips.

"Thank you." She smiled shyly, wariness still hovering around her edges. "I ran down my groceries and only had a yogurt cup for breakfast."

Before he could remark on her being so active on very few calories, she asked, "If you're into self-driving cars, how did you come to buy out the Tabor?"

"I took over the family corporation, Gallo Proprietà, when my grandfather died. We have holdings in other interests, but it's mostly hotels, restaurants, some shipping and other import-exports."

"I know what Gallo does, but that's what I mean. Self-driving cars aren't really in the company's repertoire. Why are you running a resort conglomerate if your passion lies in something completely different?"

"I was always intended to be my grandfather's successor. I took a double major in business and computer engineering because it interested me. When I left school, self-driving was still a sci-fi story, but I believed in it. My grandfather believed in me, and we all expected him to be around longer than he was. It seemed a safe bet to explore my hobby for a few years, but we lost him unexpectedly. I had to put it aside and take up the leadership at Gallo."

"Do you like running it?"

"I don't dislike it. It doesn't matter either way. I did what needed to be done." Did she realize how closely she was skating onto thin ice?

"Have you pursued anything to do with cars since then?"

Not that he admitted to anyone, having learned the hard way to keep his cards against his chest. "Why? Are you looking for another bite of technology to profit from?"

The pretty inquisitiveness that had grown in her eyes dimmed to hurt. "And here we are again," she murmured in a tone that cooled several degrees. "I can't blame you for being cynical, but I'm not my father. I'm just making conversation."

So much for a pleasant day.

"When did Stephen—?" he started to ask, since he had been wondering.

"Eight years ago." She had stopped eating to dig into the pocket of her jacket, pulling out a credit card.

"Put that away," he growled.

She set it on her phone and looked for their server.

"Put it away or I'll take it."

She scooped both phone and card into her lap, glaring at him. "I'm not going to sit here and be accused of things I haven't done."

"I liked him," he bit out, furious all over again, just like that. Hurt. Betrayed. "That's why I couldn't believe he did that to me." He picked up his wine, but it tasted sour. He'd lost his appetite, too. "How did the crash happen? Drunk driver?"

"Icy roads." Her voice held a crack, and the words gave the knot around his heart a hard, abraded yank. "I got a job at a ski hill in Banff and was moving there for the winter, so I could train in my off-hours."

"How old were you?" She couldn't be more than twenty-five now.

"Sixteen."

"Is that when you broke your leg?"

"Yes." She didn't have to tell him she felt guilty for being the reason they were on the road. He could hear it in the heaviness of her voice. Could read it in the anguish tightening her profile. That also caused a weird pang in his chest.

"It wasn't just a broken leg, though, was it?" He looked at the white line next to the hollow at the base of her neck.

"Collarbone and a punctured lung. I had six surgeries over two months, then rehab for a year. Lucky to be alive, so I can't complain."

Reeling under the idea that she might have died, he asked, "Was your whole family in the car?" He already knew they had been.

Her mouth tightened. She nodded. "Mom died instantly. I was unconscious. Dad talked to Reeve for a few minutes, tried to tell him what to do, how to stop the bleeding. Reeve was twelve and had a broken arm. He managed to climb up the embankment to flag down help. It took a while for a car to come along, but they stopped, which is why I'm still here. That's why we always stop."

The hairs on the back of his neck lifted, thinking he might never have met her if not for those strangers.

"That's why I helped your grandmother. That's why Reeve wants to be a doctor. He felt so helpless. Don't interfere in his plans, Dante." She looked him dead in the eye, hers glossy and bright. "It's not about my father or what he might have cost you. It's about helping people you and I don't even know and never will."

Dante hadn't consciously thought her brother was becoming a plastic surgeon or some other high-paying specialist, but to hear he had such a personal, karmic reason to pursue a medical degree took him by surprise. Unsettled him.

Careful, he reminded himself. Fagans were liars.

But this was too brutally real. He'd seen the scars. He could hear the agony in her voice.

"What happened after the accident? Where did you go?"

"A group home." She pulled her lightweight jacket around her. "Reeve was able to stay with a school friend. I was glad about that. They were good people. But taking him was a hardship, not that they would say so. They couldn't take me, as well. I was fine."

It struck him that he'd known her barely forty-eight hours, and he couldn't count the number of times she had assured him she was "fine."

"It was hard to see him, though. I was in Edmonton and he was in Calgary. Once I turned eighteen, I moved to Calgary, found work and an apartment. Got custody of him. We figured it out from there."

Her phone pinged and she flicked at the screen. "Reeve is home. I'm sending you the documents he scanned."

Dante's phone pinged, but he didn't look at it.

"What?" she prompted, frowning at his hesitation.

"He's had all day to concoct something," he admitted, trying to be dismissive, but he was affected by all she'd just said. Surgeries. Family broken and sent to a group home, yet she was quick to smile and offer help.

Her jaw dropped open, astonishment hollowing her cheeks. Then her eyes grew sharp and bright, brow spasming once before she looked away.

"I'm wasting my time." She stood and walked out.

If he called out to her, she didn't hear. She was too busy trying not to let on that lactic acid had set her leg on fire. She clung to the rail down the outer stairs to the ski rack, gritting her teeth.

Do. Not. Cry. He wasn't worth it. But she was dangerously close to tears, and it wasn't all physical. He kept breaking down her defenses, giving her a day fashioned straight from her most cherished dreams, then kissing so tenderly she damned near cried at the sweetness of it.

She had put a stop to that kiss, which had taken monumental effort, but she had been feeling so fragile under the press of his mouth. He could have had her making love in public, she was that susceptible to him.

She couldn't understand why or how he stripped her down so easily. She had poured her heart out about her parents, reliving the pain, trying to earn some tiny shift in his regard by conveying there had been a cost. He didn't need to punish her. She lived in torment every day. At the same time, she felt enormous empathy for him that he had lost his own parents.

Yet he couldn't even be bothered clicking his phone to glance at the albatross he had placed around her neck after she had already lost everything.

They had absolutely nothing left to say to one another. And it gutted her.

She took the more gradual green run down to the bottom, skiing cautiously and mostly on her good leg. She was shaking with exertion when she turned in her skis. Maybe some of her tremble was rage, but she was too tired to pick it apart. She just wanted to get to the bus station—

Oh, *damn*. Her backpack was in the back of Dante's SUV. Dear God, would this man never stop torturing her in one way or another?

Gathering her things from her locker, she limped outside, wondering if he had already left. She would have to wait on a bus and go to his hotel, wait there for him.

"Cami."

Her nemesis was right there, skis off, changed and everything, looking dark and glowering as a god of wrath.

"How—?"

"I took the black run."

Of course he had. "Rub it in, why don't you?" She limped around him. "I need my backpack." She was furious and hurt, most especially because he had ruined her favorite thing in the world—skiing. Today had been perfect. For a while.

She sniffed.

Don't cry!

She suddenly found herself swooping toward the sky, horizontal, as if she'd slipped on ice and was flying up, but she landed in the cradle of his arms.

"What the *hell* are you doing?" Her oversize handbag swung off her shoulder, and she thought she was going to tumble as she grappled to secure it.

He was so strong, he held her firmly until she stilled again. It felt amazing to be carried with such confidence. Strange and wonderful and terrifyingly good. She hated him, wanted to bash him, but her nose clogged with emotion and her throat stung. His virility made her weak. She felt safe, held like this. Coddled. It took everything in her to resist curling into his embrace and sobbing against his neck.

Then he spoke and his voice was so grim, he chilled her blood.

"How the hell do you know the name Benito Castiglione?"

"You read it?" She let him carry her while she searched his expression, desperate for a sign that what he had seen had changed his mind about her.

He looked worse than skeptical or remote. Hostile. Furious.

Chest going hollow, she said weakly, "I don't know him. He's just the guy who told us where to send the money and how much. Why? Who is he?"

"He *was* my patent lawyer. But he's dead. He died a few days after your family left Italy."

CHAPTER FIVE

CAMI BLINKED, TRYING to comprehend.

A tiny spark of hope danced in her periphery, wanting to believe this news meant the money was sitting in a dormant account somewhere and would be returned to her like lotto winnings. But deep down she knew that wouldn't happen. No, she knew she had lost that money as surely as she'd lost the Tabor job and her parents and any chance at a gold medal. That's how her life *worked*.

She stopped trying to think at that point.

Her life had fallen apart that many times, she simply couldn't face another level of disaster. That's why she'd gone skiing. The world looked different from the top of a mountain. Up there, she was a tiny organism on a timeless planet. For a little while, she had skied fast enough to outrun reality.

But like a deadly game of snakes and ladders, she had landed at the bottom yet again. Her emotions slithered and coiled into all the dark places she had visited over the years, which was a miasma of fear and depression. She tried to think what her next steps should be, but only found a void. Her brain was paralyzed.

She swiped at a tickle on her cheek, realizing she was crying. Dante had put her into the passenger seat of his rental, and she was leaking silent tears like a giant, pathetic baby. Searching her bag, she came up with a tissue and blew her nose, trying to scrape her composure together.

Dante pulled to a stop and she squeezed her eyes closed and open, blinking hard to see through her matted lashes. They were at his hotel.

Well, what did she expect? That he would drive her back to her apartment building? They weren't friends. She had not—despite heroic efforts—paid him back a dime of the money her father had stolen. He owed her nothing.

Her breaths grew tighter as it sank in that she had lost her chance to prove she wasn't a liar. There was no earning his good opinion now. She would only sound like more of a raving lunatic. He had a right to feel contempt toward her, but it hurt like hell that he still did.

The valet opened her door and she slid out, gingerly putting weight on her sore leg as she limped to the back of the vehicle for her backpack.

"Dante."

He turned back from walking toward the entrance. His dark glower cut her in two.

What remained of her fragile self-worth shrank further into a hard ball inside her chest. Her voice sounded fraught when she spoke, waving at the back of his SUV. "I need my backpack." She'd sleep on the floor at Reeve's. It wouldn't be the first time.

What would her brother say about all of this? She was supposed to be older and wiser, but she had messed up *again*.

This was so unfair. Everyone had things go wrong in their life, but no one's life went *this* wrong, did it? When she was trying so hard to be good and do the right thing?

"We need to talk. Come inside."

"I can't." Her emotions were barely held in check. Once she had processed all of this and figured out a course of action, she would be fine, but right now it all seemed so big and overwhelming. Impossible. Where had the money gone?

Don't be pathetic. No more tears. She bit her lip, fighting the pressure in her chest and behind her eyes.

"You need me to carry you?" His voice was gruff as he came toward her. "Do you need a doctor?"

"No. I mean I can't talk to you. It hurts too much," she said baldly, hand trembling as she swept her fingertips beneath her eyes.

A muscle pulsed in his jaw. "I want to know exactly what is going on." He put his arm around her, not really giving her a choice as he took most of her weight and drew her into the hotel.

She went because she was tired and had nowhere else to go. She needed to sit down and think, maybe get a few answers of her own. She went because, just for a minute, she needed to lean on someone stronger. Even if he hated her.

He didn't release her in the elevator. He smelled really good, like snow and pine and spicy man. She stood there dumbly against him, absorbing his body heat, barely resisting tilting her head against his powerful chest, grateful for human contact when she was feeling so hideously small and persecuted.

A moment later, they entered what had to be the platinum penthouse. It was a beautiful space with a main floor lounge in soft earth tones and buttery leather furniture, cozy accent pillows and a gas fireplace throwing off heat. There was a discreet kitchenette around the corner with a powder room beyond. Stairs led to what she presumed was a master bedroom in a loft while a wall of windows rose up both stories, overlooking the mountains. On a summer's day, four doors would fold back on themselves, opening to a terrace and letting nature inside.

"This is really nice," she murmured as she moved to look at the view turning golden with the last of the day's sun.

"Noni doesn't like stairs or she would have had it." He turned away and began making coffee, asking if she took cream and sugar while the machine gurgled.

She dug into her handbag, coming up with a blister pack of pain pills with two left. She popped them out and limped over to pour herself a glass of water, quivering under his watchful eye as she swallowed.

"Why did you ski so hard when it's not good for you?"

She had wanted to spend time with him. That was the uncomfortable truth. Her heart squeezed.

Too much about this man affected her. Pulled at her so strongly, she was now just a frayed mess of loose threads.

"I won't get another chance for a while. Make hay while the sun shines, right?"

Cami's wan smile and the way she avoided his gaze didn't strike him as completely honest, but Dante didn't know what to believe anymore. He shook his head and carried their coffee to the table in the lounge.

She followed and sank onto the sofa, then picked up her mug, wrapping her hands around it. Her nail beds were white, and the tip of her nose red. He probably should have sent her into the bath, but he needed answers. He was still in shock after seeing Benito's name attached to a letter dated a mere two years ago.

"So." He hitched his pant leg as he sat down across from her. "Explain."

"I—" The anxiety around her eyes increased. "I don't know how. I thought I'd been paying you back all this time. Not from when we left Italy. I didn't know what was going on then. Only what I told you before, that my parents kept us in the dark about a lot of it. I only knew we had to sell everything. My *skis*." She tried to throw away the remark like it didn't matter, but her voice thinned. The way her brow crinkled in a small flinch revealed how hard that had been for her.

Judging by her passion for the sport, he could imagine what a stab in the heart it had been. Almost as lethal as when he'd realized his precious design work had been copied from his computer and given to his competitor.

"I assumed later that Dad had made a lump sum payment to you, but I have no proof of that. Apparently, I don't have proof of anything." Her empty hand came up.

If she'd been in a witness box and he in the jury, he couldn't have picked apart her visage more thoroughly. The slant of her lashes, the color returning to her cheeks, the tension in her brow and the pull at the corners of her mouth.

He searched meticulously for clues as to whether she was lying or telling the truth, half thinking he should have gone with his first instinct and let her ski away and out of his life once and for all. As she had walked out on their late lunch, he had told himself she wasn't worth the head games. He was better than this. Smarter.

But he hadn't been able to resist glancing at the attachments she'd sent. The second he'd seen Benito's name and the date, his brain had exploded. He'd gone after Cami only to see her skiing away on one leg. He hadn't realized she'd cut down the beginner run until he was on the steepest one and couldn't see her. He'd caught up to her at the bottom, but he'd been worried—sickly worried—when she took so long to show up.

The effect she was having on him was as disturbing as all the rest. Part of him still wanted to walk away from all she was stirring up, but he couldn't. Not just because of this new twist with Benito, either.

He resented feeling this compelled by her. *Ensnared.* How was she even doing it?

He let his fist land on the arm of his chair as he made himself focus on the external facts, rather than trying to unravel the internal.

"Are these all the letters you've received from Benito?"

"Just the most recent. Did you see the one where I asked for a phone call with you a year ago?"

"Why? What did you want to say to me?"

"That—" She struggled a moment. "I know you don't care, but this has been difficult. Finding the money." Her tone grew raw enough to scrape at his conscience. "I was trying to help Reeve with school. I wanted to work out a different payment scheme. He said you wouldn't negotiate. That I had to stick to what was agreed or go to court."

"Agreed by whom? Your father?"

"I don't know." She looked conflicted. *Afflicted.* "I didn't know anything concrete about what Dad had done until I was out of the system and moved to Calgary. Some government-appointed something-or-other handled the probate on my parents' estate while I was still in hospital. The only records I ever saw were the papers that Benito forwarded. All I knew was that my parents had been broke. There was nothing to come to us, but the will stipulated that once I turned legal age, I could be Reeve's guardian, so I made that happen. He'd been with me a few months when the letters started arriving."

"From Benito."

"Yes." She nodded. "I was really scared. I couldn't afford a lawyer, especially for an international crime. He sent Dad's confession and that said it all. Dad was guilty and had promised to pay you back a ridiculous sum." She looked to the ceiling, as if trying to keep the moisture in her eyes contained. "I'm not *you*. I don't have a family corporation behind me with properties all over the world. I have a used anchor of a laptop and my mother's wedding band. There was nowhere for me to even begin finding that money. But I know I'm on the hook for it, since I'm pretty sure Dad took it to pay for my training. I'm not trying to dodge it, Dante. I'm just saying, you can't get blood from a stone. I've been doing the best I can."

He thought of the tiny apartment with the well-used furniture. The relic of a mobile phone and the fact she had taken over-the-counter medication, not prescription opiates.

But she was also very protective of her brother's aspirations.

"What happened after you started sending the payments?"

"I wound up overextended and got us evicted because I missed rent." Her voice was heavy with culpability. "I lost Reeve for a couple of months until I got on my feet again. He's never forgiven me for that." She sighed heavily. "Life lessons, right? The social worker was actually really helpful. Got me a grant so I could take the hospitality program and that led to my jobs with hotels and the transfer here when Reeve started going to school in Vancouver. Rent in this town is killing me, though. That's why I thought the job at the Tabor was a good move. I would finally have some breathing space, but…"

He had pressed the detonator on that.

He set the side of his finger along his lips, trying to work out whether she was the victim of a con or trying to make *him* into one. Again.

"What happened to Benito?" she asked.

"He was murdered over gambling debts, if the rumors are true."

"Oh, my God!"

"Yes, it was quite a shock. Especially as he hadn't yet filed my patents. I turned to one of his colleagues, but there wasn't much they could do except offer advice. The evidence against your father was circumstantial. They advised me I could spend years and a fortune trying to prove his guilt, and probably never get restitution, or I could settle for a confession and a promise of a settlement. Which is what I did, keeping the whole thing as confidential as possible, so as not to damage the viability of Gallo Proprietà. We were in rough shape. I had to be careful."

"I'll go to the bank tomorrow and stop my auto withdrawals, ask them to dig up what they can about who owns the account where the payments have been going and switch them to you." She touched two fingers between her brows. "I just feel like such an idiot. It never once occurred to me to check he was a legitimate lawyer. Or that he was *alive*."

Dante belatedly picked up his phone and forwarded

the attachments from her brother to his own lawyer, requesting an investigation.

"Stopping payment should flush out another communication from the fake Benito, right?" she asked.

He tilted his head, agreeing with her logic, even if he still had reservations about whether the fake Benito had been created in Italy or on her brother's laptop.

A shadow passed behind her eyes. "You're still suspicious of me. I guess I can't blame you, but... I don't know how to convince you. I don't know how to fix this. This theft has been an awful cloud that has hovered over me for years. I look back and feel so selfish. So single-minded and stubborn. So *responsible*."

She swallowed, looking ill.

He ought to revel in her self-recrimination, but he couldn't help thinking her drive was the quality a champion needed. Her lack of fear and love of speed would have taken her only so far. True achievement took grit. In fact, she probably wouldn't have recovered from her injuries if she hadn't had that blind will to overcome obstacles.

A strange regret hit him that he hadn't paid more attention when her father had spoken about her. He vaguely recalled an invitation to visit their chalet and watch a race. Dante had been caught up in his own goals and self-interest, but wished now he'd seen her when she'd been coming into her own as an athlete. They'd been well-matched today. He could only imagine how much better she would have been if she hadn't been injured. She would have been on podiums; he had no doubt.

"You were eighteen when the letters started coming?"

She nodded mutely.

A gullible age. She'd been in a vulnerable position, playing parent to her brother. He could see how easy it would have been for someone to take advantage of her. But who would know enough of the circumstances to do it? Only the main players, most of whom were dead. One of Benito's colleagues, perhaps? The criminals to whom he'd owed debts?

Was this a confession of youthful ignorance? Or a well-honed ability to manipulate?

That face of hers was the problem. She projected innocence with those earnest eyes and delicate features. Skin he already knew was soft as down. Lips like flower petals. He only had to look at her and he ceased to care what she may or may not have done. He only wanted to devour her.

Heat began to pool in his lap. He shifted restlessly.

"I really do want to compensate you, Dante. I'd do anything to have this paid off and pushed into the past."

"Would you?" He couldn't help it. The haze of sexual need was coming over him, thickening his voice.

She flashed him a stunned look, then her hands went into her lap. She stared out the windows a moment, lips pressed into a flat line, eyes holding a sheen. "Why do you keep treating me like that? I've never slept with anyone for money or clothes or jewelry. I've never slept with *anyone*. Period."

"Ha!" Now he knew she was lying, and there was something terribly disappointing in that.

She glared at him. "Why is that so impossible to believe?"

"You're twenty-*four*."

"Don't judge me by *your* standards."

"You honestly expect me to believe you're a virgin?"

"When have I had time to date? What man wants to sleep with a woman with the kind of baggage I cart around?" She flung her hand through the air. "I don't care if you believe me or not! It's really none of your business, is it? Oh, wait. That's what you keep accusing me of, isn't it? Trying to make a business transaction of trading my body for the debt my father owes you. First of all, wow. Wish I'd thought of that sooner. So much easier than working three minimum wage jobs. Second, exactly what is a woman's virginity worth these days, anyway? Maybe I *am* interested."

Cami spat out the words, hot with insult, adding bitterly, "Times have changed, by the way. It's not the woman selling herself who is reviled. It's the man who takes advantage of her."

His cheeks went hollow before he stood abruptly. She threw herself into the sofa back. He barely leaned toward her, but intimidated all the same. She held her breath.

"I don't think either of us is vile. *That* is the problem." He shoved his hands into his pockets. "I keep thinking I want to sleep with you regardless of what your father did. That makes me a stupid man. I cannot let you take advantage of me the way your father did."

"I'm not trying to! I don't—" Were they really talking this baldly? It felt as if she was stripped naked. "I don't know why I keep kissing you. I don't act like that. I swear I don't."

"If your father hadn't damned near destroyed me, I would call it what it seems to be. Chemistry. Sexual compatibility."

How romantic.

She looked out the window again, toward her first love—snowy slopes. Had it only been a few hours ago that they'd traced through powder, crossing paths to braid a scrolling line into the mountainside? It had felt divine. Like they were made for each other.

"I always thought that when I felt like this about someone it would be..." She swallowed, embarrassed. "You know," she mumbled.

"A husband? That is not going to happen." His voice turned so cold and hard it left bruises in her ears.

"Someone I knew well enough to care about them," she corrected in a voice that frayed around the edges. "You honestly think I'd want to marry you? Yeah, that would work out, with this hanging over me. Talk about selling myself into sexual slavery."

He didn't like that. His expression grew even more stony. "Be careful, Cami. I'm trying to be patient, to hear you out."

She bit back a snide, *You started it*.

"I don't want to be attracted to you, either," she admitted, feeling naked as she openly acknowledged this wild compulsion inside her. "You have been squeezing my life in an iron fist for years. You have wiped out what little I have managed to build here, in the first place that felt like home. I have no future, not unless you grant me one. *You* have all the power, Dante. All I have is a thread of self-respect, earned by trying to do the right thing all these years. But you're taking even that, acting like my...my very natural reaction toward you is some kind of commercial product." She stood and looked for her handbag. "I can't keep doing this."

"You're not leaving."

Her racing heart thudded to a halt in her chest. "Excuse me?"

His expression was remote. "I'm going to the bank with you tomorrow."

"Fine. I'll meet you there."

"I'm not risking you taking off before morning."

"You don't even trust me to show up to one of the most important meetings of my life?"

"I do not."

Her heart stumbled all over again. "So you'll what? Lock me in here?" The thought of spending more time with him was terrifying. She had just admitted to attraction, and if she knew one thing about this man, it was that he didn't let an opportunity to get the better of her slide.

"So melodramatic," he drawled. "I'm extending

my hospitality." Folding his arms, he added dryly, "Which includes the private jet tub upstairs."

Her muscles were so stiff, she very nearly whimpered at the lash of temptation that went through her. "That's just mean."

He moved to the house phone and said to a concierge, "I need a bag brought up."

CHAPTER SIX

DANTE DISAPPEARED TO talk with his grandmother, so Cami felt safe enough in the moment to use the tub. She needed time to think all this through and might as well work out her kinks while she did.

He turned up as she was about to enter the tub, making her heart dip and roll.

The room was humid with the scent of cedar off the paneled walls. The darkness outside disappeared behind the gather of steam against the window and the jets hummed beneath the burble of the churning water.

"I didn't realize you were joining me." She self-consciously kept her loosened robe over the ridiculously functional one-piece bathing suit she wore. It was bargain store brand in a flat blue, not sexy in the least.

Which was a good thing. He was only keeping her here because he didn't trust her, not because they had chemistry. *Sexual compatibility.*

She wished he hadn't named it. She dearly wished that was all it was for her, but her reaction to him was as emotional as it was physical. He was arrogant, yes, but he also showed great love for his grandmother. He had an admirable sense of duty to family, and his odd moments of protectiveness were positively swoon-worthy.

Her wobbly defenses disintegrated further as she took in his broad shoulders and naked chest, flat abs and tiny red racer's suit. Something sharp and hot struck deep in her intimate places. The scrap barely covered his bits, revealing more than it concealed of the bulge at the top of his muscled thighs, making her curious as to whether he'd stay contained if he became aroused.

She yanked her gaze to the water, hot all over. With a flustered move, she threw off her robe, leaving it on the hook as she slipped into the water as quickly as her protesting muscles allowed.

He lowered into the other side of the round tub, mouth quirked in amusement as he spread his arms along the edge.

"What?" she asked crossly, suspecting he was laughing at her.

"Maybe you are a virgin."

She wasn't about to have *that* argument again. It hurt too much to hear him sound so cynical about it.

"Thank you for this," she made herself say, trying to steer toward a less intimate topic. She crooked her knee so the jet was aimed directly at her thigh. "A warm shower wouldn't have been enough."

"How did you start skiing?" His tone was lazily curious. He was relaxed, which should have put her at ease, but she was too sharply aware of him. Of herself and the swirling sensations in her middle and deeper that had nothing to do with the water.

"Mom raced." She tried to gather her scattered thoughts. "But she started late and didn't qualify for more than a few provincial games. She put my brother and me on skis from an early age, though."

"She supported your aspirations."

"A million percent."

"It wasn't you who drove the move to Italy, then. She wanted it for you."

"They both did, but once my coach said I should go, I pressed them until they made it happen." That was why the weight of guilt sat on her so indelibly. "What happened to your parents?"

"Boating accident. There was a storm."

"I'm sorry." Their gazes connected, and she felt that brief click that was more than sexual. Their stories were different, but they shared the same pain.

He broke the contact, slouching so he could rest his head back and look to the ceiling. As he sank down, something grazed her hip, making her start with a gasp. She realized belatedly it was his foot and glanced up in time to see his head come up. His mouth twitched.

His expression didn't change, but she felt the side of his foot nudge her hip. He was trying to get another reaction out of her while keeping that innocent look on his face.

She stared right back at him, deadpan, ultraconscious that things were happening below the surface they were refusing to acknowledge.

"Are you Catholic?" she asked abruptly, talking so she wouldn't think of the way a narrow line of hair had arrowed from his navel to the snug band of red drawn low on his hips. Damn. Now she was thinking about it.

"Not a very good one."

"Because you believe in birth control? Sex before marriage?" Why had she gone *there*? *Shut up, Cami.*

"Those are sins I confess to," he drawled. "Not something I 'believe' in."

"What do you believe in?"

He grew more serious. "Taking care of family. Loyalty. Responsibility."

She nodded agreement.

"Carpe diem, because you might not live to do the things you otherwise put off. Paying debts."

"Of course." She stiffened and lifted her leg out of the jet, setting her foot on the bench and massaging her thigh where her muscle felt itchy from the vibration of the forced water.

"Are you angry that you can't ski the way you want to?"

"Yes." She heard the rigidity in her voice. The resentment. "Are you angry you can't design cars?"

"Yes." For a long second, they shared another look of understanding, reflecting each other's frustration, connected at a soul level.

"But you could pursue cars in the future. You have the resources. Even if you wait until your retirement, it's always something you could go back to. I can't even try for senior games. My best hope is the occasional day like today."

He skimmed across to her, making her gasp at his sudden closeness.

His strong hands took possession of her thigh, so unabashed she instinctively tried to pull away, but he held on and dug his fingers into her tense muscles. "I didn't expect it to cost you so much. You should have said."

"Oh." She almost cried at the intensity of his touch, but the relief that came behind the pain had her shuddering and melting.

A very long time ago, she had had professional massages. His firm thumbs dug into her aching muscle with just the right amount of pressure. His hands kneaded their way up her thigh and down to her knee, then began working upward again.

"That feels really good."

She gave herself up to it, fingers gripping the edge of her seat, letting him find the tension and release it. Press and ease back, circle and stroke. Swirls of desire fluttered into her belly as his attentions went on. She tried not to reveal her reaction, even as secretive parts of her pulsed in yearning and her mind turned to thoughts she could no longer suppress.

His hands climbed her thigh again and she held her breath, imagination dancing toward "what if." What if he touched her *there*?

"Cami."

She barely heard him, his voice was so low. She dragged her eyes open and realized she had let her legs drift open. His hands were at the very top of her thigh, his thumbs tracing the leg of her bathing suit.

"I don't want you to be embarrassed by the way you react to me."

"Look at who we are. It's so wrong." It was true, yet she was turned inside out by the stillness of his hands, aching with longing because he was so near and yet so far.

"It's not smart." His arms gathered her to sit across his lap. She was so weak, she floated into place, entranced by the glow of desire in his eyes. "But it's not wrong."

She didn't see a difference, but she stopped caring. She lifted her mouth and he covered her lips in a hot, unhurried kiss, one that made her feel as though she was drowning, but delirious at being swept away.

Her butt cheek pressed into— He was hard. Really hard.

On the rare occasions she had made out with a man, this was always what made her alarm bells go off. She always ended things before her date started thinking she wanted to go further than she did.

She and Dante had barely got started, though. Her one arm crooked alongside his rib cage, and the other hooked around his neck so she could twist her torso into facing him while they kissed. And kissed and kissed.

Oh, he knew how to kiss! Five o'clock shadow abraded her chin, but she couldn't get enough of his lips. They were smooth and full, like an exotic fruit that was an aphrodisiac. The more she gorged on him, the more she wanted. She sought his tongue with her

"4 for 4" MINI-SURVEY

We are prepared to **REWARD** you with 2 FREE books and 2 FREE gifts for completing our MINI SURVEY!

You'll get...

TWO FREE BOOKS & TWO FREE GIFTS

just for participating in our Mini Survey!

Dear Reader,

IT'S A FACT: if you answer 4 quick questions, we'll send you **4 FREE REWARDS!**

I'm not kidding you. As a leading publisher of women's fiction, we value your opinions… and your time. That's why we are prepared to **reward** you handsomely for completing our mini-survey. In fact, we have 4 Free Rewards for you, including 2 free books and 2 free gifts.

As you may have guessed, that's why our mini-survey is called **"4 for 4".** Answer 4 questions and get 4 Free Rewards. It's that simple!

Thank you for participating in our survey,

Pam Powers

To get your 4 FREE REWARDS:
Complete the survey below and return the insert today to receive 2 FREE BOOKS and 2 FREE GIFTS guaranteed!

"4 for 4" MINI-SURVEY

1 Is reading one of your favorite hobbies?
☐ YES ☐ NO

2 Do you prefer to read instead of watch TV?
☐ YES ☐ NO

3 Do you read newspapers and magazines?
☐ YES ☐ NO

4 Do you enjoy trying new book series with FREE BOOKS?
☐ YES ☐ NO

YES! I have completed the above Mini-Survey. Please send me my 4 FREE REWARDS (worth over $20 retail). I understand that I am under no obligation to buy anything, as explained on the back of this card.

☐ I prefer the regular-print edition 106/306 HDL GMYF   ☐ I prefer the larger-print edition 176/376 HDL GMYF

FIRST NAME   LAST NAME

ADDRESS

APT.#   CITY

STATE/PROV.   ZIP/POSTAL CODE

READER SERVICE—Here's how it works:

own, wanting that earthy contrast of textures, the deepening of intimacy.

She loved how he shaped her body, rocking her chest against his. She wiggled, encouraging the play of his fingers over her like he was a sculptor learning the shape of her spine, the curve of her backside, pausing to gently squeeze, then moving on, leaving a trail of inflamed desire in his wake. Her own hands splayed to stroke the supple skin across the cage of his ribs, the balls of his shoulders and the flex of his pecs.

Then, somehow—and she didn't understand why she did it or where she got the courage—she found his shape through the thin fabric in his lap. Drawing back, she looked into his face as she delved beneath the tight elastic waistband and closed her fist over what felt like smooth, wet satin stretched over a column of hot marble.

His breaths grew ragged as she explored him.

With his lashes so low, she could barely read the avid hunger in his gaze. He skimmed his hand between her thighs and eased her bathing suit aside, baring her to the hot water and the sweeping stroke of the backs of his fingers.

It was delicate, a taste, not a meal. Need sensitized her and a sob of pleading left her.

He kissed her as he fondled with more purpose, parting and exploring, making her twitch under the onslaught of sharp sensations, wet and dangerous, intimate and sure.

"Move your hand," he whispered against her lips, then covered her mouth in a deeper kiss.

She moaned a protest, wanting to keep touching him, but curled her arms around his neck, pressing her breasts to his chest.

He lifted his head enough to release a breath of laughter against her panting mouth. "I meant move your hand *on* me. Stroke me."

Oh. What an idiot! She ducked her head into his neck, aware by the shake that went through him he was laughing at her.

He was also removing her bathing suit! All the skin that had been covered turned silky and alive. It was a rebirth of sorts, making her feel new. He left her suit on the edge of the tub as she slid her hand under the water again, finding him, feeling him pulse in her touch as she gripped him. Caressed and explored.

He did the same to her and she quickly lost the plot.

With a helpless groan, she threw back her head, offering her mouth. He smothered her with his kiss. Ravaged her. Slid a long finger inside her and rolled his thumb, causing her to fill the room with cries of acute pleasure as he took her over the edge.

Had she given him any pleasure at all? She made a belated effort to squeeze him, but he stopped her, arms going hard around her as he stood in a sluice of water.

She was hot and lethargic and so incredibly aroused. Naked as he skimmed his gaze over her, inventorying her pale skin and white scars, the pink nipples that stood up even in the sultry heat of the spa.

As he looked her over, insecurity edged in. All she could think was that the ache he'd left in her hadn't been enough. She wanted a sharper stretch, a harder possession. She wanted him to make love to her. This man, the one who made her tremble. If he decided she didn't measure up...

"Are you really a virgin?"

"Yes." Was he going to call her a liar again? Reject her? She would die.

His nostrils flared. "Do you want to stay one?"

Stop? "No."

"Good." He carried her to his bed.

"We'll get the blankets wet." She started to sit up as he set her on the mattress.

He made a growling noise. "It doesn't matter." He stripped his microscopic suit and left it on the floor as he crawled over her, pressing her onto her back.

She tensed with nerves, hands going to his shoulders, not in protest, but caution. He was very intimidating, so big and muscled and *hard*. Like tensile steel beneath the press of her fingertips, but hot, so incredibly hot as he covered her wet, chilled skin with his own. They were both damp enough there was tack as he settled on her, sealing them together.

She had never been under the weight of another human, a *man*. Naked and trembling. She considered herself a strong woman, physically fit, but she was suddenly very aware of herself as small and slight. Vulnerable.

He could crush her. Hurt her. Break her in two.

He shifted his weight onto one elbow, heavy thigh pinning hers.

"When I saw this that first time, I wanted to kiss it," he said with a light trace of his fingertip against her collarbone, where the healed skin was sensitive and the bone still tender to the touch. He touched his lips to her scar, and her eyes fluttered closed under a swell of deep emotion, chest expanding so she could hardly breath.

How was this even happening? He was like a sorcerer. Brute force wasn't necessary. He cast a spell and overwhelmed her with her own sensuality. She was weak and conquered and she liked it. He didn't trust her and she probably shouldn't trust him, but as he nibbled his way up her neck, sending tingles through her nape, into her scalp and down to her nipples, she entrusted herself to him. Maybe the aggressive feel of his erection against her hip made her anxious, but it was the nervous excitement she had once experienced before a race. Anticipation of being wild and free.

Stroking her fingers through his damp hair, she brought his head up so they could kiss. She couldn't get enough of his mouth, and he seemed to like hers. Hunger met hunger and she found herself arching into him, naked breasts swollen and hard, all of her wanting to convey her surrender. It was instinctual. Elemental. *Mate with me.*

His big hand cruised up her waist and gathered her breast, then he lifted his head to watch his thumb play across her taut nipple, keeping up the teasing even when she gasped and writhed at the intensity of the sensation. Streak after streak of wired sensations

sent pulses into her loins. Then he dipped his head
and drew on her so strongly she gave a keening cry.
Sexual heat flooded through her, piercing her sex.
Any droplets of water left on their bodies evaporated
in a sizzle that was nearly audible.

She stroked him with her whole body, loving the
feel of his skin against her palms and belly and inner
thighs. As her legs opened, he settled into the space,
slid down and pushed her legs farther apart. *Claimed*
her with his mouth.

Waves of pleasure worked their way through her as
he stroked her with his tongue, the onslaught making
her quiver with tension. With agonized need. She lost
all inhibition. Gave herself up to whatever he wanted
to do to her. She *belonged* to him.

Just as her peak neared, he rose over her, making
her gasp in agonized denial. A plea hovered on her
lips, tightened her chest, but she couldn't speak. His
fierce eyes met hers, and she knew that *he* knew she
was his. Utterly and completely. It was in the flare
of his nostrils and the hard curl of satisfaction across
his mouth.

But there was something else there. A glimmer
of cynicism. He didn't quite believe she was a virgin. It was this infernal response of hers, clouding
his view of her.

Reservation should have struck. Maybe resentment or refusal, but perverse anger hit instead. Let
him take her and *see*. That would show him. Then he
would know, once and for all, that she wasn't a liar.

Wouldn't he?

Either way, he was doing it. Reaching a long arm to the night table to retrieve a condom. As she watched him roll it on, a very feminine hesitation rose in her. Was it going to hurt?

She was about to find out. He settled so he was poised to enter her. She studied his face, tense and flushed and severe. He pressed and she instinctively stiffened, tightening all over, fingers splaying on the searing plane of his chest.

"No?" His gaze flashed to hers, white-hot as lightning.

"I'm sorry," she murmured, agitated. "I'm nervous." She made herself relax. Moved her hands to his sides, still wary.

He said something in Sicilian. His frown eased. He pressed a soft kiss on her lips and caressed where he was trying to invade. As a wash of pleasure returned in a sensual rush, she moaned and relaxed. He pressed into her.

It did hurt, but not a lot. A strong pinch and a determined stretch. A tremendous *fullness*. Incredible and incredibly intimate. He seemed to have a lot to offer. He propped himself on his elbows, fingers in her hair as he withdrew a fraction, then pressed in again. Each time she thought that was it, he did it again, sinking deeper each time.

She was shaking, thinking this wasn't the dreamy romantic act she had always imagined, but very, very real. Everyone in the world did this, but it was the first time she was doing it, and it was more physical than she had expected. Carnal. Intense.

There was no hiding anything from him when connected to him this way. Her eyes might be closed, but she couldn't hold back her small gasps. He had to know she was trembling, even though he shook, too, shoulder blades flexing under her hands.

She opened her eyes and saw his lips pulled back with strain. A muscle pulsed in his jaw, and his breath hissed through his teeth. Just as she thought she couldn't take any more, he settled on her, belly to belly, fully seated inside her, and opened his eyes to look into hers.

"Bedduzza," he breathed, thumb touching her temple. "Hurt?"

A tear had leaked out the corner of her eye.

"It's just really… I didn't expect it to be this—" Intimate? Important? "It's overwhelming." She was different now. He was her first lover, and she would remember forever that he looked so remote as he possessed her this way. Fierce to the point of frightening. Yet tender enough to kiss away her tear, leaving her feeling strangely divine.

"You're killing me." He eased her legs around his waist and sank a fraction deeper, then he cupped her jaw. She could feel the tension in his grip. The restraint. He said something else in Sicilian before he covered her mouth in a kiss. Sweet and lavish, but with a purpose. He wanted to incite her passion and did.

Soon she was responding, moaning into his mouth, thinking a kiss was so much more significant when bodies were joined. She could feel him pulsing inside her. It made her needy and frustrated. She sank back into that world of sensation he seemed custom made to deliver to her.

He began to move.

It hurt, but assuaged at the same time. She didn't know what to do, but her body did. She undulated with him, finding the rhythm that fed the fire. They seemed as completely attuned to one another as they had been on the hill, meeting and parting, returning again and again to each other. Creatures of the earth doing earthly things.

As his tempo increased, so did her greed. Her arousal level. Somehow she was there again, ready to peak, clinging to him with every fiber of her being. Making agonized noises of acute pleasure while he moved faster and bit out something that could have been an order or a plea.

She couldn't hang on any longer. She let go and plummeted into the abyss, falling apart even as he pulled her in with him. His hips thrust deep and his cries underscored hers as they clung through the paroxysm that exploded, then melted them into a heap of boneless flesh.

Dante lay on his back, forearm flung across his brow, distantly aware of noises in the bathroom, but his brain was barely functioning. He didn't bother trying to discern what she was doing. He had managed to roll away long enough to remove the condom, noticed blood and handed her a tissue. She'd released a mortified gasp and retreated to the bathroom where she had left her things when she had undressed for the hot tub.

He stayed on the bed, sorry he'd hurt her, but wrung out by the best sex he'd ever had. His organ was still tingling. All of him was. His entire body was damned near singing like a choir.

He hadn't even meant to kiss her. When he had ordered her to stay, he really had been thinking he only wanted to keep an eye on her. Go to the bank with her tomorrow. Unravel the Benito mystery.

Okay, maybe sex had been hovering in the back of his mind because they'd acknowledged the elephant. *I don't want to be attracted to you, either.* Wanting her was a betrayal of himself, but fighting this attraction had proved to be beyond him. They were consenting adults, and he had thought she was as experienced as any millennial. He hadn't believed her about being a virgin. Not really. Not when she responded like she'd made love a thousand times.

He'd been as gentle as he could, once he discovered how tight she was, only really believing she was new to the act when the deed was done. When she'd had him in a vice of pleasure so acute it bordered on painful and a tear was trickling from her eye.

That fragility of hers had been the only thing that kept him this side of savage while a storm of possessiveness engulfed him. Maybe the imposition of restraint had made the build that much greater, he didn't know, but definitely he was affected by the knowledge he was the only man who'd ever enjoyed that passion of hers. Something truly base and barbaric wanted to be the only man who ever would. Their mutual release had been cataclysmic. Beyond his experience.

So good he already wanted to make love with her again.

So self-destructive. She was a lying, thieving Fagan.

Except she hadn't lied about being a virgin. That meant he had to give a little more credence to her other claims. He absorbed that, disturbed. Suppose she *had* been paying him back in good faith. That meant there was a criminal making victims out of both of them.

She came out of the bathroom, footsteps heading toward the stairs.

He dropped his arm and saw she was wearing her miniskirt and droopy pullover. Did she have nothing else? He was sick of seeing her in that. He should take her shopping, as he would with any lover.

Is that what she was?

"Where are you going?"

She paused with her hand on the ball of the newel. Her teeth released her bottom lip into a small pout. Her brow crinkled with uncertainty. "To Sharma's."

An uncomfortable skip of alarm went through him along with his newfound possessiveness. His muscles tensed, ready to spring from the bed and drag her back there. "You're staying here, with me."

If he had any remaining doubts that she'd been a virgin, they were snuffed by her tortured profile as she looked away. He'd never witnessed such discomfort with post-lovemaking rituals. He always tried to keep things very friendly with his lovers, if casual. This wasn't casual, though. He and Cami were inextricably linked by their past and now by a unique experience. Her first time.

An edgy uncertainty wound through him. How would she remember this? How would he?

He would never forget her; that much he knew. The profoundness of this encounter was still hitting him, breaking down and rebuilding things inside him.

She kept her face averted, but he read her defensiveness. Underlying insecurity. Should he soothe and reassure? What message would that send?

As the silence protracted, she flinched and started down the stairs.

"Cami." He came up on an elbow.

She paused. Her shoulders fell. "I can't keep doing this, Dante."

"Neither can I," he lied, deliberately misunderstanding her. "You have done the impossible. Exhausted my libido."

"I'm sure you say that to all the girls," she shot back.

Ah. Now he understood. "You knew *I* wasn't a virgin." He curled his arm beneath his head and relaxed once more. "Frankly, you want your first experience to be with someone who knows the ropes."

"But I didn't expect it to be with a stranger. I barely know you! And I didn't expect to feel so…" Her jaw firmed as she faced him with a hint of cynicism. "Well, I guess I'm not supposed to feel anything, am I? That's how these things are supposed to work, aren't they?"

Why that stung, he didn't know. He came up on his elbow again.

"Come here." He patted the edge of the mattress. When she hesitated, he said, "Do you need me to come get you?"

She tightened her mouth and warily came across to perch on the side of the bed.

"Did I hurt you?" That question was burning a hole in his brain.

"No." She brushed at a fleck on her skirt. "I mean, a little. The normal amount, I suppose." She shrugged, blushing. "I'm fine."

He liked women, liked flirty ones who were sweetly perfumed, soft and indulgent of his needs. He liked to indulge them. Spoil them and pet them and enjoy the warmth of their bodies against his own.

This one was prickly and wary and someone he should not trust. Nevertheless, she invoked a rueful remorse in him with her tart, "normal amount." He wished it was none.

He gathered her up and rolled so she was beside him on the bed, all elbows and resistant stiffness. She made a face and lifted her head off the pillow. "It's wet."

He threw it away and dragged a dry one into its place. Then he watched her try to avoid his gaze, expression grumpy. She wasn't trying to get away, but she didn't relax.

"I didn't believe you," he admitted, suspecting that

was the real source of her desire to flee. "You're very sensual. That wasn't your first orgasm in the tub."

"Oh, please. I know how my own body works." She rolled her eyes.

"And now *I* do." He let that sink in, watching the pink that deepened in her cheeks beneath the fan of her lashes. "Does that bother you?"

"Yes. I get the feeling you've made a study of how to get that sort of reaction from women, and I'm just the latest specimen you've collected."

Nice. "So you regret giving me your virginity."

"A little." She reached to touch a button on the headboard. Sighed as she dropped her arm back to her side. "You already have all the advantages. Now you have this to lord over me, too."

"Why give it to me, then?" It was the other question sizzling in his brain.

Her mouth twisted. "I wanted to. I've never had much personal choice, so I take it where I find it."

He caressed her jaw, gently taking hold of it, feeling her tense, but he wanted to see into her eyes. They were brimming with anxiety. Defenselessness.

He stroked the backs of his knuckles into the warm flesh beneath her jaw and below, down her throat, enjoying the way she shivered and softened. The *response* of this woman. She made him feel like a god. He wanted to strip her naked and bury himself inside her all over again, just to reach that level of supreme euphoria.

But she was so new to this, she didn't see how much power she had over him, which was a good thing.

He kissed her. Just long enough to find her response. To reassure himself it was there and, yes, maybe to reinforce his power over her. His hand was still on her neck, and he felt the throb of her pulse and the vibration of her helpless sob as it emanated.

He lifted his head and she ducked her chin. "What about you? Regret?"

"Yes."

Her breath rushed out and her eyes filled, stunned with injury. He touched her swollen mouth with his thumb, and she drew her lips in so the pad of his thumb rested on a flat line.

"I don't sleep with employees or anyone else with whom I have other types of relationships," he explained. "I prefer to compartmentalize. Keep lines drawn so feelings don't color facts."

She withdrew from his touch completely, sliding backward across the mattress. "And what you feel for me is hatred, isn't it? It bothers me that I made love with someone who hates me."

His chest tightened. Hatred was a damned slippery fish to hang on to right now.

Her lashes dropped and the corners of her mouth were heavy. "Maybe I deserve it, since it's my fault my father stole from you, but it still hurts." Her subdued voice held a lot of pain. "I said I'd do anything to get rid of that cloud over me, but I don't think this did anything except scrape away what little respect you might have had for me. So now I'm embarrassed and would prefer to leave."

"That option is not on the table."

"*Why*? I said I was a virgin and I was. Doesn't that earn a shred of trust?"

He couldn't let her go. That was the bald truth.

"Until I unravel this Benito mystery, I can't let my guard down with you." He knew that much, but he also knew he already had. "It will take some time for the bank to investigate, so you'll stay with me until we have some answers."

"*With* you. Here. In your bed." Her voice thinned to something that might have been resentment, but held an echo of longing, too. "Doing what? Paying off Dad's debt? How much did my virginity knock off the total, anyway? I'm such a terrible negotiator. I should have asked *before*."

She was throwing darts because she was hurt that he still mistrusted her. Her words still managed to get under his skin. "Do you want to put the past behind us or not?"

He meant that her snippy attitude wasn't helping, but she only railed on in the same vein.

"Let me guess. You'll also leave my brother alone if I sleep with you?"

"Sure." He had no intention of going after her brother. It was easy to agree.

Her eyes narrowed. "Exactly how many payments are you expecting?"

"We'll make love 'the normal amount,'" he quoted her pithily, through a smile that was more clenched teeth and growing ire. "But I won't make demands right now, if you're feeling delicate. Or salty."

"Oh, no," she said with a hot crackle in her tone.

"If I'm going to get this debt off my back *on* my back, let's make sure I get it done."

"You really think you can shame me, you hellion?" He tangled his fingers in her hair, holding her pinned for gentle, gentle kisses. He teased and tantalized both of them until she was clinging to his lips with her own, moaning in frustration because his hand in her hair wouldn't allow her to lift her head and increase the pressure.

Her hands moved with agitation across his back, one snaking to try to take hold of his reviving shaft, but he caught both her wrists in one hand above her head. He used his free hand to caress her breast, taking his time to really appreciate the shape of her, the heat he could discern even through the knit of her pullover, the dainty circle of her areola and the exquisitely sensitive peak that jabbed beneath his thumb pad, making her breaths grow ragged.

She wriggled and made another noise of growing ardor, lifting her mound into the weight of his thigh where he pinned her hips to the bed.

"Dante," she gasped.

"I'm not a monster, *bedduzza*." He moved his hand to skim back and forth across her waist, stealing inch by inch beneath her pullover, feeling her tense stomach quiver and jump beneath his tickling caress. "Tell me you don't want this and I'll stop."

She made a tortured noise. "You'll make me want it anyway. Won't you?"

He found her braless breast and cupped the underside. She arched, trying to fill his palm. Her nipple stood like a shard of glass beneath the fabric of her top. They both ached for him to bare and lick and suck that taut tip, but he held off, nearly blind with desire. "If you really want to earn my trust, Cami, you have to be honest about what you want right now."

Her breath exhaled on a trembling hiss. "You," she confessed.

He gave her what she asked for.

CHAPTER SEVEN

CAMI WOKE ALONE. As she sat up, she breathed out a low, wincing breath. She was *so* sore. The jet tub might have forestalled some of the stiffness from skiing, but just as she hadn't let a few aches and pains hold her back from enjoying the slopes, she hadn't let it slow her down with Dante, either.

She buried her face in her hands, appalled. The man really did have an extraordinary libido, and apparently so did she.

Now she was paying for that physical activity. With a little whimper, she made her way into the shower, feeling only marginally better when she dried herself with aching arms. Her nipples were incredibly sensitive and even brushing her teeth was a tender exercise, making her look for bruising around her mouth. Her lips were chapped, but what had that man done to the rest of her? At no point had he been brutal, but he had been thorough.

And she'd loved it.

She was a sex fiend!

It was embarrassing, but as she thought of the way they'd come together again and again, the way his hands had felt on her body—his *mouth*… She was aroused all over again. Yearning and wanting another clash of flesh to flesh.

She clenched her eyes against her reflection, aghast by the longing that overcame her, fresh and sharp. Glancing at the closed door of the bathroom, she wondered if he was still in the suite.

Be honest about what you want.

What *did* she want? Romantic love was not something she had been able to afford, quite literally. After losing their parents, her brother had been her world. Mentally, she'd felt miles ahead of men her age, and the few who had bought her coffee or a plate of pasta had been quickly scared off by her financial situation and depth of responsibility.

She had tucked away dreams of finding her soul mate like a pressed flower in a book, rarely remembered and even more seldom examined.

Dante was *not* her soul mate. He was her instrument of sexual awakening, but all she could expect from this relationship was maybe some sort of closure between them on her father's debt, one way or another.

That stupid debt! She glanced at the time and realized the bank would be open soon. She dried her hair, then dressed in jeans and a snug, waffle-knit shirt.

"Dante?" she called from the top of the stairs.

Silence.

She limped down to the main floor and had a very cursory look for a note—and painkillers—but found neither. He hadn't texted either, but he'd left a key

card. At least she wouldn't be locked out if she ran
to the lobby. Her leg throbbed like it was newly broken. She really needed something.

Ugh. She didn't want to be the first to text. What
should she say? *I'm up? Where are you?* Far too needy.

She was in the elevator before she settled on her
message.

Do you want to meet me at the bank?

He responded promptly.

We'll go together. Wait for me.

The reply pinged into her phone as she made her
way across the lobby toward the gift shop. How long
would that be? she wondered.

In the same moment, she felt a prickle of awareness, like the sun came out and found every inch of
her naked skin.

A soft, aged voice said, "Cami!"

With her head bent over her phone, she had nearly
walked right past Dante, Bernadetta and another couple, all sitting in the casual dining lounge where the
buffet breakfast was served, finishing their coffee.
She was separated from them by a row of ferns.

As Cami took a startled inventory, her gaze tangled with Dante's. All the wicked things they'd done
to each other cascaded through her mind's eye, turning the middle of her chest into a furnace that radi-
ated heat through the rest of her.

He looked like their intimacy was the furthest thing from his own mind, staring at her with a flat, hostile stare that silently conveyed, *I told you to wait for me*.

The sweet excitement of seeing him again drained away before it had fully formed, leaving her hollowed out by his disapproval.

"Dante said you decided to stay in Whistler and wouldn't be coming to Vancouver with us. He didn't say you were staying at our hotel." Bernadetta looked questioningly to her grandson.

He took a sip of his coffee, which struck her as buying time.

Cami's blush turned to one of indignation, then scorn, as it impacted her that he was having break-fast with his relatives and not only hadn't invited her, he didn't want them knowing she'd spent the night with him.

"I'm staying with a friend," she provided, turning her attention to Bernadetta, even though she suspected Dante would consider her words a lie. They weren't "friends."

The old woman introduced her niece and husband. "Cami is the young woman who was so kind to me the other day."

Cami brushed that aside, saying, "I'm glad I could help, and it's very nice to meet you. Thank you again for the day of skiing, but I'm sorry. I'm on an errand. Safe travels." She leaned to return Bernadetta's light embrace and got the hell out of Dodge, so humiliated she could hardly bear it.

* * *

Dante caught up to Cami at the gift shop cash register, about to pay for a bottle of extra-strength headache caplets. She looked spectacular in curve-hugging jeans. The legs were tucked into her tall boots, accentuating the slender thighs that had hugged his hips last night while she gasped and moaned beneath him.

Her hair, that cloud of silk that had erotically grazed his skin and imprinted the scent of almonds and crushed flowers in his psyche, fell in shiny waves down her spine, drawing his eye to how narrow and delicate her shoulders were.

Leaving her this morning had been a struggle. It took everything in him now not to set possessive hands on her hips and draw her into his front, so he could shape her breasts as he molded her back into his frame.

He was obsessed, which was exactly why he'd made himself sit with his cousin and grandmother when his mind had been several floors up, making love to Cami all over again.

Yanking his libido to heel, he took over her purchase, signing it to his room.

"What are you doing?" she asked stiffly.

"What are *you* doing? You could have asked the concierge to deliver these."

"Hardly." She pried open the cap as they walked out of the shop.

"What do you mean?"

"Hotel staff are run off their feet. I'm not going to play prima donna and ask for something I can get for myself." She glanced toward the dining lounge. "Where's Bernadetta?"

"They've left."

She detoured into the buffet and helped herself to a glass of water, washing down two tablets, before dropping the medicine into her handbag.

"Would you like breakfast?"

"Bit late for that invitation, isn't it? No, thanks," she pronounced with disdain. "I'm going to the bank."

"The phone didn't wake you," he pointed out. "You seemed to need the sleep." He could have used another two or three hours himself. They'd bordered on debauchery. Every single minute had been fantastic.

"You didn't ask me to join you once you knew I was up. In fact, you were horrified that I happened by. Sorry to be such an embarrassment." Her heels clipped loudly across the tiles.

"Quit being so dramatic." He paced alongside her. "It was the opposite. Noni is so smitten with you, she didn't stop talking you up over breakfast. She *wants* me to continue seeing you."

"So then why—? Oh." She halted as they exited to the covered portico.

He handed his ticket to the valet, then pushed his hands into his pockets. Judging by the way Cami paled and stared stiffly ahead, she was connecting the dots.

"You don't want her to think we have a future," she summed up after several long, fuming minutes. "Because we don't."

"She's very anxious to see me married," he confirmed. "But I have no desire to tie myself down. It's not personal."

"I'm sure," she muttered, stepping forward as his vehicle came to the curb.

He didn't owe her explanations, but spoke once he was behind the wheel, pulling away. "I've never met a woman I trust enough to even consider marrying her. I can't bring myself to risk the family fortune again."

"It's one bludgeon after another with you, isn't it? Now it's my fault you can't fall in love and marry? My father's betrayal means you can't make your grandmother happy and produce an heir for everything her husband built? I'm sorry, all right? I'm sorry I ever wanted something as useless as a gold medal. Turn left at the next light."

He signaled and changed lanes. "I didn't say it was your fault."

"You *implied* it." She stared out her side window, but swung her head around a moment later. "And somehow, I'm supposed to be so good in bed that you get over that? Exactly how many orgasms will it take to open your heart enough that your one true love can walk in?"

"I don't know, Cami. How many until you quit acting like a martyr? Is this your bank?" He recognized the logo from the bank transfer she had shown him that first night.

"Yes. And what is that supposed to mean? I'm not being a martyr!"

"People are allowed to want things for themselves." He swung into a parking space. "I wanted to be on the cutting edge of a new technology. That doesn't make me a bad person who deserved to have his work stolen. You keep acting like wanting to ski competitively is a crime. No. It's just a dream, and people are entitled to go after their dreams. You think I don't respect you, but I'll tell you something. The way you skied yesterday was badass. It takes guts to send yourself down the side of a mountain at those speeds. Quit apologizing for being good at it. For liking it and wanting to prove how good you were."

She flinched at the word *were*.

"You do blame me, though." Her fingers picked at the stitching on her handbag. "You fired me."

"I did. But how I let the past affect me is my choice." Not that he'd consciously faced that before it came out of his mouth. He'd let Stephen's betrayal eat away at him, only becoming aware of how destructive it was since meeting her. "Your desire to ski didn't make me the way I am. You're not that powerful," he concluded dryly.

She was powerful enough to have him reassessing his reaction to her father's theft, though. He absorbed that while watching her thumb work against the stitching of her bag.

"I just really miss them," she said in a very small voice. "I know it's backward logic, but if I believe that making a wrong decision can cause someone's death, then making the right choices will keep others alive. Like Reeve. I don't want to believe death is just random bad luck. If that's how things work, how could I stop it from happening again? I don't want to be that powerless."

He sighed and reached to cover her hand, stilling her twitching fingers and weaving his between them. "It is a terrifying fact that life is nothing but shaken dice." He hated that particular reality himself.

"Thanks," she muttered, extricating her fingers and reaching for her door.

He felt the loss, the sense of having disappointed her, acutely. His reaching out in comfort, offering a hand-holding, had been the least sexual, yet most intimate act he'd ever shared with a woman.

And she'd rejected it.

The bank meeting was even less fruitful than Cami had expected, and she had prepared herself for heart-wrenchingly low results.

The manager was nice enough. She sat with them for about ten minutes, took Cami's information, but told her the file would have to be referred to the bank's fraud department. Someone would be in touch.

She stopped future payments and very help-fully printed out the history of Cami's transfers to the Benito account, which subtotaled to a sickening amount. Cami could have financed her brother's bachelor degree by now.

She didn't know if she was supposed to feel foolish or vindicated as Dante glanced at it, but mostly she felt disregarded. He'd spent half the meeting texting.

Was she playing the martyr? Not consciously, but in case he had forgotten, he had taken her apart and put her back together last night. Several times. A tiny bit of regard this morning didn't seem like a big ask. He was flaying her to bits.

"Are you serious about my staying in Whistler?" she asked as they exited the bank. "Because there's clearly no point."

His head came up from his phone, distracted frown sharpening. "What do you mean?"

"You couldn't care less what the bank is doing and don't want to be seen with me, so—"

"I'm talking to the bank right now. Not this one, but the head office of Benito's bank in Milan. I know one of their VPs. I sent him an email this morning and didn't expect to hear from him because of the time change, but he's visiting his wife's family in America, so he's already started checking into it. He does not look kindly on the family bank being used as a laundry by criminals. He's established that the account is owned by a numbered company and says these transactions are often hidden by bouncing them through a few channels, trying to dodge detection. He'll keep digging."

"Oh." Her feet glued themselves to the sidewalk.

"Oh, indeed. As for not wanting to be seen with you, I explained why that's awkward with my grand-mother. I was going to ask you if you would like to go to a club tonight, though. I bumped into an acquain-tance over breakfast. He owns Afterglow. Said he'd put me on the list." He quirked his brow as though suggesting his acquaintance was being pretentious.

Afterglow was *terribly* pretentious. It was where

all the celebrities went when they came to Whistler. She had secretly always wanted to see inside, but clubbing was one of those luxuries she'd always wondered about, but couldn't afford. Like everything about this man, his invitation tempted her simply for the chance to spend more time in his company, but she was so disconcerted, she could only shrug self-consciously.

"Do *you* want to go?"

"We can't make love nonstop," he said with a smirk of untold arrogance.

"Evidence to the contrary," she muttered.

He let out a bark of laughter, something that made standing on this sidewalk with him the most amazing place to be in that moment, contentious relationship or not. It made her yearn for something more with him. Something truly meaningful.

His phone pinged and he glanced at it. "I have to drop by the Tabor. Can you amuse yourself until lunch?"

He didn't threaten to tie her to the bed in his suite, she noted, but simply assumed she would stay with him.

She folded the printout she still held, thinking of the restitution she had failed to make, despite her best efforts. She really did want to put the past to bed, but wasn't sure if his bed was the place to do it. Walking away wouldn't allow for any sort of peace between them, though.

"I'm going to look for a job. See if I can scare up a place to live so I can stay here instead of moving to Vancouver."

A shadow of something moved behind his eyes, dissolving the humor that was lingering there.

He nodded. "Good luck. See you at lunch, then." He planted a kiss on her that left her heart pounding and walked away.

When they returned to his suite at the end of the day, a rack of dresses and accompanying accessories filled the lounge.

"What—?"

"You need something to wear to the club."

A dress. Not a wardrobe!

"I bought a new top to wear with my miniskirt." She'd found a steal on a sequined halter at the consignment store and showed it to him.

He made a face that said *meh*, and opened a bottle of wine.

"What's wrong with it?" She'd done a lot of hand-wringing today, wondering if she was making the right choice, but kept coming back to wanting him not to hate her. To see that she was doing the best she could.

"Indulge me," he said, jerking his chin at the dresses while pouring glasses. He seated himself on the sofa as though settling in to watch a sports final.

"You want me to model for you? That's rather objectifying, isn't it?" She tried to be indignant, but a secretive part of her was titillated.

"I call it foreplay, but if you'd rather not…" He shrugged, but the slant of his mouth suggested genuine disappointment. Enough to make her want to laugh.

"Is this your thing?" she asked, casting him a curious look as she fingered through the dresses. "Your kink? Do you go to strip clubs?" There was so much about him she didn't know.

"No. But I like to see beautiful women in beautiful clothing. I think that makes me one hundred percent normal heterosexual male. Vanilla, even."

"I'm not beautiful," she said absently, holding a dress of gold fringe against her front, glancing at him for his reaction.

He nodded approval, saying, "You are."

She glowed under the compliment, even as she denied it. "Prettyish, at best."

She slipped behind the rack and unzipped one boot, then the other.

"That's not me fishing for reassurance. Just honest self-assessment." She was pear-shaped, not hourglass. Her lashes needed about a pound of mascara to thicken them up to "average." Her face was on the roundish, girlish side, not elegant or aristocratic. "I have decent skin and nice hair, but I'm no supermodel."

"Women are idiotic, setting ridiculous standards for themselves," he said as she skimmed away her jeans and top.

"As foreplay goes, yours sucks."

She heard his choke of laughter, then a growled "Yours is excellent. You're making me insane, hiding back there. Get out here."

She bit back a smile, suddenly taking great enjoyment in this flirt and play. This lighthearted teasing made her happy. Optimistic. She hugged the dress to her bare front for a moment, deciding to stop trying to figure out where they were going and embrace what they had. She slowed her movements, giving him a show beneath the rack of clothing by stepping one naked foot through the dress she was trying on, then the other, then very, very slowly shimmied it up her bare legs.

"You'll pay for that," he warned.

"I'm starting to worry we'll need a spreadsheet for all the debits and credits." Holding the front of the loose dress, she came around, growing nervous as she showed herself. She padded toward him and turned so he could zip her.

He set aside his wine and sat forward. "Lift your hair."

She did, felt the dress draw close around her, then his heavy hands settled on her hips. Every single fringe seemed to tickle across her cheeks. Her entire backside began to tingle. Little teases of arousal fluttered through her loins and upward to her breasts.

"Heels, *pi fauri*," he said absently and sat back.

Her whole body warmed as she moved away and chose a pair of gold sandals with an ankle strap and a four-inch spike.

"I'll help you," he said before she could sit to put them on.

His voice was very low and intent. He opened his thighs so she could set her foot on the cushion between his knees. He took his time, caressing her arch and ankle before putting the shoe in place, then taking care with closing the buckle. He motioned for the other.

She had trouble balancing, knees nearly unhinged so she had to grasp at his shoulder.

"Walk to the window," he commanded softly.

She did, slowly, feeling his gaze on her like a million suns. Maybe she didn't consider herself beautiful, but in that moment, she felt glamorous and exotic. Prized.

It was strangely empowering. She struck a provocative pose as she looked over her shoulder at him, back arched, hip cocked.

"I don't like this one," she said haughtily. "I want to try another."

He sat arrested with his drink halfway to his mouth. His voice was velvet and leather, thick and smoky and sensual. "By all means."

She tried on one in a rich burgundy in a fabric light as air. The spaghetti straps barely held up the cups over a deep cleavage. The skirt was a handkerchief cut with high slits.

"What do you think?" She fluttered the skirt to reveal and conceal her legs nearly to her hips, deliberately teasing, though she wasn't sure which one of them was more affected. Her body was warm and her muscles growing lethargic with sensuality. "Too high school prom?"

"The black shoes, I think." His voice was a silken ribbon sweeping over her and coiling tight, squeezing her breath.

"No," she defied with a shake of her hair. "I want

to try something else." She checked in with him and liked the way his mouth was deep at the corners, his eyes narrowed with absolute focus on her.

"The blue, then." It was a strapless mini with silver embossing, tight as a second skin.

"*Now* the black shoes," she stated, sauntering to collect them.

"Bring me that bag." He nodded to a pink bag with silk handles and a logo for designer lingerie that Cami hadn't noticed.

The wicked flutters in her abdomen grew as she brought the items across to him.

He plucked the tissue from the bag and spilled jewel-colored silk and lace across the cushion beside him, fingering through the items for long moments before taking up a miniscule scrap in midnight-blue with an edging of black lace.

She reached for it.

"I'll help. Hold still."

She was paralyzed, barely breathing as he hitched forward, legs opening so his knees bracketed hers. He grazed his flat hands up her thighs, beneath her skirt. The tightness of the knit in the skirt ironed his palms to her skin. His fingers slid across her hips, then hooked into the edge of her very boring, white cotton underwear. He eased them down until they fell in a bunch at her ankles.

"Step." He held the new ones for her.

She was losing track of which one of them was in charge. She obeyed, bones so weak she had to brace on his shoulder again. She quivered under the erotic scrape of lace up her thighs, at the way she thought she could feel the abrasion of his fingerprints against her skin.

He smoothed the thong into place, running thorough fingertips along her hips to ensure there were no twists. His thumbs followed the triangle across the front, causing a pulse of anticipation that was nothing but molten heat, so intense she nearly sobbed.

"I'm going to ruin them," she whispered.

"I expect I'll be ripping them off you very soon, *bedduzza*," he said, very slowly drawing his hands from beneath her skirt and gently tugging her hem into place. "Would you like to walk for me? Or shall we change your shoes first?"

"What do you want?" She could barely stand while he sounded quite composed.

"I would like to change your shoes."

She swallowed and set her foot on the cushion, skirt riding up and no doubt affording him quite a view as he first removed the gold ones, then eased the black velvet heels into place, tightening the ankle strap of first one, then the other.

As she started to draw her foot back to the floor, he tightened his hold on her ankle, urging her to stay exactly as she was.

Her hair fell in curtains around her face as she looked down at him. The helplessness she felt in that moment was terrifying, making her worry this was a huge mistake, yet she couldn't deny herself or him.

"I don't think you're ruining them," he said, watching her as he lazily caressed up her inner thigh to the damp silk. "I find your reaction incredibly exciting." He drew the fabric away from her folds. The backs of his knuckles swept her damp flesh once, twice, then he gently parted and explored more thoroughly.

"I don't…think." Couldn't think. Not at all. She swallowed and swayed. "I can't stand."

"No? How are you feeling otherwise? Tender?" He did wizardly things that made her bite her lip and moan. "All day I've been thinking about last night. How incredible it was. How delightful you are."

She didn't expect him to say such things. Her eyes teared up. She teetered and he caught her, pulling her down so her knees straddled his thighs. They kissed, hot and urgent. She fairly attacked his mouth and only lifted her head because she felt him searching for her zipper and wanted to get her hair out of the way.

As her dress loosened, he brushed down the bodice. In virtually the same motion, he slid his hands under her bottom, shoving her skirt to her waist as he urged her to stand on her knees so he could suck her nipples.

They were ultrasensitive, and she had to set a hand on his jaw, urging him to be gentle.

He threw his head back and his expression was full of rapacious hunger and barely contained restraint. He slid down enough to dig in his pocket, then clutched the condom packet in his teeth while opening his fly.

He very easily dispatched her brand-new, worn-for-a-minute underpants with a twist of his wrist. A second later, she followed his guiding hand to take him in.

The ferocity in his eyes was her whole world as he

filled her, inch by inch of granite thickness, heavy hands on her hips urging her to take up the rhythm they both craved.

Clutching at the back of the sofa, she rode him, lost to sensation. To pleasure. To a climax that had her arching and releasing helpless cries as she shuddered and quaked.

"Beautiful," he said through clenched teeth. "Do it again."

Dante had had mistresses before, but none like Cami. She was proving to be a delightfully quick study on the physical side of their arrangement, but remained a reluctant virgin to the rest, which was an exciting yet frustrating combo.

As his new manager for the Tabor prattled in his ear, trying to impress him, he watched Cami talking to his HR manager for the chain. The Tabor's dining lounge was decorated for its gala opening with a sea and sky theme. Clear balloons stood in bubble strands under sparkling star lights set off by drapes in evening blue. Cami should have blended in, but she was stealing all the attention in an ethereal gown that made her look like a water sprite. It spilled down her figure in shades of green, backless and draping her ass to perfection. Short sleeves stood up on her shoulders, made of a netted fabric that stood up like delicate wings, increasing the impression Cami was a magical creature sent to enchant him.

Her hand lifted briefly, touching an earring again. She was terrified of losing them, which was part of that adorable, aggravating lack of assumption she exhibited with their relationship.

"I didn't see they'd included accessories," she had said when he presented the green sapphires with a matching oval-cut pendant. "They chose well, didn't they? Suits the gown."

She had just finished curling her hair into big, lazy scrolls of dark coffee and rich auburn shot with threads of gold. They had fallen in ribbons around the shoulders of her hotel robe, making his fingers itch to muss them.

"It's from me," he had informed her dryly, astonished that she was still taken aback by his attentive touches. "Lift your hair."

"When did you have time to shop? Is this from the boutique in the lobby?" She had turned to the mirror as he clasped the necklace.

"There's a shop near the Tabor." He'd mentioned the name of the local jeweler.

"These are *real*?" She'd spun, clutching at the pendant like it was going to combust. "But just on loan, right? As advertising or something? Did they tell you what I should say?"

"They're a gift." A modest one by his standards, but the best the place had. Yet she had reacted as if he'd poured his mother's wedding necklace into her hands.

A darkness had passed behind her eyes before she'd shielded them with her thickened lashes. Her eyeliner tailing to a point at the corner of her eye, framing lids shaded with green and gold.

"You've given me too much already."

A handful of off-the-rack dresses and some underthings that were more for his pleasure than hers were hardly going to break the bank. Neither was the pretty bauble, yet her reluctance to accept it had niggled.

"You don't like them? They can be exchanged."

"I'm worried something will happen. I've never worn anything so expensive."

"Except skis?" Elite equipment cost a small fortune.

She conceded that point with a hitch of her shoulder, but then added in a mutter, "This isn't how this is supposed to work. I'm already in your debt enough."

He *hated* talk like that from her. It cheapened every press of her mouth to his body, every cry of ecstasy he wrought from her, making him think she was only here because of her father's theft, not because she wanted to be.

"I'm quite happy with the return I'm getting," he'd drawled, not quite disguising his aggravation. "Let me see."

Her gaze flashed once to meet his in the mirror, then she'd set aside her palette of rouge and turned, knuckles white where she clutched the edge of the vanity. Each time the past rose between them, the same flare-up happened between them, pushing them apart. He grew defensive, despite being the one who'd been wronged. She took on a haunted look that turned knife blades in his middle. He'd begun wondering what the hell he was doing, keeping her here with him like this, and had the unpleasant feeling she was wondering the same.

The bank had yet to supply any answers, so they had no way to resolve this impasse. His solution was to burn away misgivings with the white-hot passion they stoked in each other. Not the best coping strategy, but it was the one he'd reached for in that moment as he'd slowly, deliberately, tugged her belt loose so her robe fell open.

He'd drawn in a long breath as he drank in buttermilk skin framed in snow-white silk, pouted nipples hardening under his gaze to tight strawberries that made his mouth water.

He'd carefully centered the platinum-set stone on her breastbone, then lightly grazed his fingertips along the edges of the robe, spreading it farther, watching a flush burn down her stomach and thighs to the fine hairs of her thatch. He could practically smell her body readying for him. He'd dipped his head to taste one nipple, then the other.

"Dante," she'd whispered, pique dissolving into the tone that prickled his scalp.

He was ready in an instant, thick and hard inside his boxers. It took one casual twist of his wrist to free himself. Then he had hitched her onto the vanity top, dipping his knees to enter her.

"Condom," she'd gasped.

"I'll pull out." He couldn't wait. Thrusting into her was a dive from an arctic wasteland into the heat of a simmering hot spring, so intense it made his back sting.

But good, fiercely good. He'd cupped his hands under her butt, cushioning her cheeks from the unforgiving edge of the vanity. She'd wrapped her legs around him and kissed him as he thrust.

He had never gone bareback before. The sensation was *too* good, sending shivers racing up and down his spine. She'd braced her hands behind her so she could arch, offering her throat, meeting his thrusts. Her breasts bounced with each impact. He'd lifted his gaze to his reflection in the mirror behind her, saw something approaching desperation in his expression that was too disturbing to confront and looked to the way her face contorted with the agony of sexual need instead. Need for *him*.

He'd increased his rhythm, trying to give her as much pleasure as he could. He felt the vise-like grip of her start to twinge and ripple. Her moans of enjoyment became sobs of abandoned delight. A growl of torment built in his throat as he'd held back his own release while he continued thrusting, hard and fast, into the powerful clench and shudder and pulse of her sheath. She was so exquisite he was quite sure he would die. She was going to kill him, head thrown back in surrender, bare heels against his ass finally easing as her panting breaths slowed into helpless bliss.

He pulled out and exploded across her stomach, straining under the force of it, completely taken apart and never likely to be the same.

His wet forehead hung against her damp shoulder,

both of them shaking at the cataclysm. He lifted his head and they looked at each other as they came back to themselves, strangers who'd nearly been mowed down by the same train and were now indelibly linked by the experience.

With muscles that trembled, he had helped her find her feet and reached for a hand towel, drying her himself. The pendant had swung across the tops of her breasts, reminding him why they'd come together in such a frantic, unrestrained coupling.

"You're my date," he had muttered, hearing the gruffness of postorgasmic gravel in his tone. "I have to look as wealthy as I am or rumors will persist that the Tabor is struggling. Say, 'thank you,' Cami."

"Thank you, Cami," she had repeated with an acrid pang in her voice. She immediately grew abashed as she touched the pendant, saying with more sincerity, "Thank you, Dante. It's beautiful."

But she hadn't met his gaze.

Now they were on that date, and he was still reeling from the encounter. Perhaps she was, as well. An introspective frown had persisted in her expression all the way here.

It bothered him. When had he ever concerned himself so deeply with what a woman might be thinking about a necklace he'd given her? If she didn't like it, she could return it. Sell it.

But he wanted her to like it. He wanted her to think of him when she wore it. Of the way they made each other feel. Every. Single. Time.

Damn, this evening was interminable. He glanced at his watch, still needing to give his speech and shake a few hands before he could have her alone again.

He knew what was really bothering him. He only had two more nights with her. That dwindling sand in the hourglass grated. His agile brain had already rearranged his schedule a dozen ways, looking to fit in an extension of his time here. What he'd really like was to bring her back to Sicily.

"Dante." The male voice, familiar as his own, had him turning in surprise.

"Arturo." He embraced his cousin with warmth. "What are you doing here?"

"Saving you. Again. What the hell are you doing?"

Cami could hear what Karen was thinking as she skimmed her speculative gaze down the dress that had cost more than either of them made in two paychecks put together, then took in the stones dangling from her ears and neck.

It's not like that, Cami wanted to say, but she was growing more and more sickened with herself because it was *exactly* like that.

Somehow, she had convinced herself that she and Dante were a normal couple. Dating. Lovers. It wasn't costing him anything to let her stay in the room with him. She had cooked for him twice in the kitchenette. They were getting to know one another and putting the past behind them.

But while her infatuation was growing into something more genuine, something she didn't even want to name because it was so vast yet elusive, he seemed quite comfortable withholding himself from all but their intensely passionate encounters. She was offering her heart. He was offering pillow-cut stones. Sharing showers and meals was not true sharing.

When he had given her this jewelry, relegating her firmly to "mistress," she had thought she might as well be sleeping with him to pay off her father's debt. Clearly he viewed sex with her as a commodity of one kind or another. It was more than lowering. It was a scorn of the heart she was leaving wide open in humble offering.

"I'm glad things are working out and you've found another position," Karen said, drawing Cami back to their awkward conversation where Cami had been trying to explain how she was on the arm of the man who had fired her so ruthlessly.

She had come over to thank Karen for helping her land the job she was starting next week. It was a night manager position with lousy hours, but beggars couldn't be choosers. Karen had kindly provided a statement that pulling the job offer to run the Tabor had been an internal decision, not a reflection of Cami's qualifications.

"Were you able to keep your apartment?" Karen asked.

"No, but I have some good leads."

"Where are you staying, then?"

"With a friend."

Karen's gaze flicked toward the bar where Dante had gone, promising to send over champagne.

Cami felt the shame that had been sitting like a knot in her chest climb her throat, reaching toward her cheeks.

"I should get back to my date," she murmured. "Good to see you. Thanks again."

All she was thinking was that she wanted to escape Karen's speculation, only noticing as she approached that Dante was talking to a man who looked like he could be his brother. He was equally handsome and well-dressed in a bespoke suit, with a five o'clock shadow and a similarly smoky tone in his voice.

He was speaking Sicilian, but as she approached Dante from behind, he looked at her over Dante's shoulder with the kind of lurid male assessment that made any woman's skin crawl.

She faltered.

Dante turned to spear her with a hard gaze.

The man switched to English.

"I don't care how good the sex is. You're under-writing a Fagan. Again. Please tell me you haven't forgiven her father's debt."

Cami felt the color drain from her face while her jaw practically landed on the floor. "Who *is* this?"

"My cousin. Arturo." Dante had spoken of him with affection more than once, but aside from being easy on the eye, she saw nothing to like, especially when he spoke again.

"I'm the man who put up his own money when your father stole Dante's. Perhaps you'd like to compensate *me* in kind?" His vile gaze skimmed down to her breasts and lingered.

"Arturo," Dante ground out, but as admonishments went it was damned thin. Meanwhile, he was looking at her like he had that first day in the lobby of this very hotel, like he couldn't believe she had the gall to exist.

"This was your idea," she reminded him. He had *made* her stay with him.

"I'm sure revenge has been very sweet, given that figure," his cousin continued, making her want to punch him in the face, but she couldn't stop staring into Dante's dark expression. "You can be forgiven for thinking with your belt buckle."

"Is that what it was?" she demanded in a voice that shrank. All of her was feeling small in that moment, so belittled she began to well up. She had been trying so hard to earn his trust, she hadn't thought to question his motivations. Her throat hurt like it was being squeezed. "You just wanted revenge?"

"What else is he getting beyond a good time?"

"Shut *up*!" she told that horrible man.

"That's enough," Dante said at the same time, but she couldn't tell if it was directed at her or his cousin. His jaw pulsed, and he reached for her arm. "Let's talk."

She evaded, backing away. "Let's not."

People were staring. Some might even have overheard and the entire room now thought she was exactly what she had argued from the beginning she was not—a woman who could be bought.

And why shouldn't they see her that way? She stood here in a gown and jewels Dante had paid for.

She was staying in his hotel room, eating food he provided for her.

She shook her head, hating herself so much in that moment she wanted to claw out of her own skin. Every single time she went after what her heart wanted—

Dear God, *no*. She couldn't feel anything toward him. Refused to allow it. No. It would kill her to be in love with him when this was only—

Biting her lip so hard she tasted blood, she gathered up her skirt and hurried out.

Cami swept out with her head high, but Dante could still see the sickly shade she'd turned. It matched the gown he had purchased in a week of what was starting to look like foolishly besotted behavior. He couldn't even defend it, unable to explain how he had let it escalate to a public parade of his own poor judgment.

"We all have our weaknesses," Arturo said as Dante fought an urge to go after her. "Yours is a desire to believe the best in people."

"She wasn't asking for any of this," Dante growled, accepting the neat whiskey his cousin handed him and knocking back half of it. "How did you even know I was seeing her?" It was a juvenile reaction, as if his cousin's interference was the problem, not the fact he was sleeping with the enemy.

Arturo seemed startled by the question. He sipped his own drink.

"I saw the post on Noni's timeline showing the two of you had gone skiing. The family grapevine is abuzz with her praises of Cameo Fagan." He ran his tongue across his teeth as though the name left a bitter taste. "I thought I should check in. That's all." He slid a sly look Dante's way. "Was she worth it?"

His cousin had a base sense of humor at the best of times, but it came across as particularly misplaced today. Especially when he snorted under the look Dante cast him.

"You are well and truly hooked, aren't you?"

He almost told his cousin that Cami had been a virgin. That her honesty about that had allowed him to begin to believe in her. He rubbed his thumb along the curve of his glass, thinking of the exquisite pleasure she had given him again and again.

But no more.

His world turned so bleak in that moment, he barely restrained himself from shattering the glass with his bare hand.

"She's been trying to pay me back, sending money to an account supposedly owned by Benito Castiglione."

Arturo's brows went up. "There's a name I haven't heard in a long time. He died, didn't he? Years ago?"

"Yes, but that's why—" Dante felt like a gullible idiot, trying to defend her. "Where would she even get that name to throw it at me?"

"Old paperwork of her father's?" Arturo guessed. "They're a resourceful bunch. I'm just glad I was able to stop you losing more than a few grand in trinkets this time."

"Sir?" The event planner who had organized this

evening's festivities approached with trepidation. "Would you like to give your speech now?"

Not even one little bit. Dante felt as though noxious fumes filled his lungs, but he made himself go through the motions of finishing his evening, ignoring the avid looks from the staff and honored guests, smoothing over whatever ripples his small scene with Cami had created.

All the while, he was mentally combing through the moments when Cami had challenged his view of her, searching for the point where he turned from man into mark. The very beginning? When she helped his grandmother? Kissed him? Fell apart under his touch in the hot tub?

He grew more and more furious with himself, more ramped for the inevitable confrontation when he arrived back in his suite.

"She'll have cut and run with the goods," Arturo said. "Which is good. You don't want her hanging around, trying to convince you of her innocence."

He *had been* convinced. That was the problem.

"Do you want me to come with you?" Arturo shadowed him all the way to the door of his suite. Dante dismissed him with a snarl of impatience.

What had transpired between him and Cami was many things, but it was above all private. He pushed in and knew before the door had shut that the suite was empty.

What he didn't expect was to find her gown on the floor of the lounge, as though she'd shed it the second she'd entered, heels kicked off beside it. The jewelry he'd given her was on the coffee table. The only shoes missing by the door were her knee-high boots.

As he climbed the stairs, he discovered there was little satisfaction in finding all the lingerie he'd given her still in the drawers and all her new dresses, some still unworn, hanging in the closet. Even the pretty scarf with her name painted in calligraphy, which he'd bought while they enjoyed the town's street fair of local artists, was still here.

Her well-worn backpack, her battered laptop and her toothbrush were gone, but the hotel shampoo was still here. She'd taken only what was undeniably hers.

He ran his hand down his face, wondering whether he'd given her too much credit or not enough.

His phone pinged and an email notification came through, advising him Cami had just sent a transfer—in the amount she'd been sending to Benito.

CHAPTER EIGHT

One month later...

DANTE SAW THE email notification and knew without opening it that it was another payment from Cami. Her third.

He rejected it exactly as he had the other two. Damn her! Every time he almost managed to push her from his thoughts—

Who was he kidding? She was there *all the time*, acting as a bar of comparison that made every other woman who crossed his path too short or too tall, too polished or too loud, too quick to make assumptions, too slow to get to the point. Too insincere and not able to laugh. Not possessing a laugh he could stand to hear.

Those were the days. At night, he woke so hard he hurt, dreams of making love to Cami dissolving into the harsh reality that he was alone in his bed and would never feel her beneath him again.

Leaning his knuckles on his desk, he gritted his teeth and told himself it was over. *Let her go.*

His PA buzzed through. "Signor Donatelli has arrived."

"Send him in." Dante clicked off his phone and moved around his desk to greet his guest.

They were distantly related through the marriage of Vito's sister, but often crossed paths in business. Gallo had worked with the Donatelli investment bank several times, so he and Vito were well acquainted and enjoyed a comfortable friendship.

"Are you holidaying? This is a long way to come for a house call," Dante said as they sat down with fresh espresso.

"It's a delicate matter." Vito steepled his fingertips. "One I thought best handled in person. It's taken a lot of digging and once I had an answer, I asked Paolo to confirm it. I wanted to be absolutely sure before speaking to you."

Vito's cousin was the president of the bank, which attested to the seriousness of the matter. Dante frowned.

"This is about the Benito account?" Dante sat back, trying to relax, but it was impossible. "I don't think I want the answer any longer."

Let sleeping dogs lie, he had thought each time he recalled that Vito had not been in touch. Dante didn't want to know that Cami had followed in her father's footsteps with skimming whatever she could from him by stringing him along as his reluctant mistress.

What *had* she gained, though? That was the part that drove him craziest.

"I am quite sure you do not," Vito said, tight smile revealing the ruthless man well disguised behind a picture-book family that included a stunning American wife and two young children. "But Paolo and I cannot, and will not, allow our bank to be used for crimes."

Vito's wife had been implicated in one herself. That's how the pair had met. She'd been exonerated, but it was the type of smudge that had only made the Donatellis that much more vigilant with their bank's reputation.

"Paolo is speaking with the authorities today. This is a courtesy call, since you were the one who made us aware of the situation."

An image of Cami behind bars flashed in his mind. "What will it cost me to quash it?"

The words left Dante's lips before he could stop them, but the idea of Cami going to prison was beyond anything he could stomach. He shot to his feet as though he could physically reach her through the email in the phone he'd left on his desktop, somehow shielding her.

"We can't, Dante." Vito's tone was both quietly regretful, in deference to their friendship, yet impassively hard. "This sort of thing could take down our bank. He has to be stopped."

"*He?*" Dante spun. "We're talking about Cami Fagan. Aren't we?"

"She's the victim, yes." Vito nodded. "But Arturo is the criminal who has been representing himself as Benito and taking her money."

How the hockey playoffs were still on when summer tourists were invading the city, Cami didn't know, but she didn't complain. She needed the tips, and this working-class pub, with its big screens and loyal regulars, was brimming with generous fans.

She was tending bar and still run off her feet. At least they mostly drank beer, which meant about a million draft pours, but not a lot of time-consuming mixed drinks. Wings and margaritas night was a nightmare.

Either way, dropping a full tray of clean glasses was *not* helpful.

She did it anyway, when she turned from the pass-through and saw Dante at the end of the bar, looking right at her. He wore a leather jacket, sunglasses and a five o'clock shadow. His mouth was a grim line that sent a numbing sear of adrenaline shooting to her fingertips and toes.

I'm not ready, was her only thought before the tray hit the floor in front of her toes. The smash crescendoed above the din, and shards of glass peppered her pant legs.

The crowd roared as if she had scored a goal.

Her shift partner in the narrow space, Mark, said, "Nice job, kid," and reached past her for the second tray, then continued filling orders, double-time.

Cami did what many a server had done in such battle conditions. She swept the glass into the space behind the garbage bin, silently promised a proper clean up later, put the broom away, washed her hands and got back to work.

She was shaking like she'd been through a war, though. Or was still on the battlefield. *What was he doing here?*

Trying to ignore Dante was impossible, but she gave it a go, continuing to work, but taking a moment to get Mark's attention. "See that guy at my end of the bar? Can you serve him?"

"You got it, kid." Mark was a student friend of her brother's, which was how she got the job. "He wants to know what time you're off work," Mark said after providing Dante a beer.

"Half past get out of my life," she muttered, but didn't expect Dante, or even Mark, heard her. The music wasn't audible over the din of voices and sportscaster calls, and the servers were yelling to be heard across the narrow, scarred wooden top of the bar.

She would have to talk to Dante at some point, though. She had faced that two days ago, when she had used an over-the-counter test and learned her life would be intertwined with his forever.

Or not. It was still early days. Things happened, not that she wished for a miscarriage, but that was pretty much how her life always seemed to go, especially if something good had come along.

Was an unplanned pregnancy "good"? She hadn't had time to process it, just knew that either way, it was a disaster of some proportion. She had expected to have time to put a plan in place before she had to face him. Never in her wildest dreams had she expected him to come looking for her. Why was he even here? She so wasn't ready to talk to him yet!

She threw herself into work, feeling the loss acutely when Dante disappeared. Had it been an accident, his coming upon her? Maybe he didn't want to see her, which now made her perversely anxious to speak with him.

Minutes later, she spotted him where he'd found a seat and nearly dropped another glass. For the rest of her shift, each time she glanced over, he was looking in her direction.

When the game finished and patrons filed out, leaving free seats at the bar, he took one, saying, "Cami."

That voice. That *accent*. How was this man her complete undoing in every way?

"Mind walking me home?" she asked Mark as the servers came up with their last call requests. "Or should I text Reeve?"

"I'll walk you home," Dante said in a low growl. "My car is parked outside your house."

"Stalker," she started to say, then did a double take as she realized how truly awful he looked. When he wore stubble, he usually cleaned it up around the edges, but this looked like two days without shaving. Or sleep. His eyes were sunken pits, his hair disheveled, his face lined with weariness.

Not Bernadetta. She had been running a damp cloth over the marble top of the bar, but stopped. "What happened? Is your grandmother—"

"She's fine. But I have to talk to you."

She flinched at the granite in his tone and went back to her closing rituals. "You need to accept my transfers."

"It's about that, Cami."

Of course it was. She had stupidly pined for him

all this time while he was here to talk bank balances. *Again.*

She shook her head, but when the lights came up, she said good-night to Mark and the rest of the staff, collected her purse and the fleece she'd stolen from her brother, and let Dante hold the door for her.

"What?" she prompted as they started down the sidewalk. Her guilty secret quivered deep in the pit of her belly.

"This is a terrible neighborhood," he said tightly, glancing into a dark alley as they passed.

"I didn't ask you to come here."

Grim silence was his reply.

She tried not to feel anything, but words, so many words, crowded her throat. She had had enough time to reflect on their affair and realize how badly she had been fooling herself, thinking they were friends. Or something. Maybe being a virgin had made her susceptible to seeing more than was there, but even before the blow up with Arturo, she had begun to realize she was nothing more to him than a paid companion. It had hurt *so badly.* His resurgence of suspicion had been a final nail in the coffin.

What would he think about her pregnancy? She didn't know how to tell him. Didn't think she could face his reaction. There was zero chance it would bear any resemblance to happiness.

She brushed a wisp of hair from her cheek with a shaky hand. "Where's your cousin?"

He drew a long, deep, pained breath.

"Never mind," she muttered. "I don't even care. He

did me a favor. You were treating me like— The whole thing was toxic and never should have happened."

I don't mean you, baby. She had to fight placing a protective hand over her stomach.

Dante swore and ran a hand down his face, not disagreeing.

She swallowed, focusing on putting one foot in front of the other when his next words had her stumbling.

"Arturo is negotiating a plea deal while investigations are underway into his bank fraud, industrial espionage and ties to organized crime. He's the one who did it, Cami. Not your father."

"What?"

Dante caught her elbow to steady her.

That tiny touch sent yearning shooting through her, blanking her mind for a millisecond.

"I don't understand."

"Neither do I." She heard the rage in his voice and the pain that underscored it.

His touch tightened briefly, then he nudged her into motion. She walked on in stunned silence, afraid to believe. She couldn't even try to comprehend what it meant for her, him, or them.

All of them.

"My father is innocent? That's what you're saying?" she finally had to ask. To hear it aloud.

"Yes."

"But he signed a confession."

"Desperate people do desperate things." He wasn't just talking about her father.

Would he think that's what this baby was? An act of desperation on her part?

They arrived at the dilapidated house that had been converted to four separate apartments a generation ago. The landlord was decent enough. Leaks were fixed and there was always heat, but he didn't put a penny into it that he didn't have to.

A lot of students lived in this area, along with some struggling single parents and yes, some drug users and ne'er-do-wells. Cami had made do in places like this before without shame.

But Dante's rented town car stood out like a gleaming, manicured thumb from a weathered work glove, making her embarrassed of her circumstances. She was at an utter loss as to how to react to any of this.

"Is your brother up? I want to talk to him, too." He reached to open the gate and hold it for her. The chivalry disconcerted her. She dumbly led him around the cluttered side of the house to the stairwell of their entrance.

She tried the door and found it unlocked, which Reeve often did when she was due home. He was in his room and called, "That you?"

"Yes. Can you come out?"

"Lemme finish this."

She hung her brother's fleece on a chair back as Dante came in behind her.

He closed the door and pushed his hands into his pockets, taking in the shabby furnishings and the corner shelf she'd claimed as a makeshift closet. Her backpack stood beside it. Her bedding was folded and stacked on the end of the sofa.

"That's where you sleep?" he asked, glancing from the lumpy cushions back to her with an accusatory glance.

She ought to be feeling superior. Vindicated. Instead, she felt less than ever. She folded her arms, muttering, "Don't judge, Dante. You're in no position."

"I'm aware," he stated flatly, and took in the clean dishes by the sink, the cupboards long past needing painting, the mismatched furniture. "This is how you live? How you've been living all these years?" He met her gaze for one second before looking away, deep emotion contorting his face. "It makes me sick."

Her heart tilted on its edge and she wanted to say, *Whose fault is that?* But she could see he was in the throes of disbelief and betrayal as much as she was. She didn't want to feel compassion. He didn't deserve it. But she still suffered for him. A desire to reach out, emotionally and physically gripped her.

"I can't imagine how difficult this is for you," she murmured. He'd always spoken about his cousin with such warmth.

"I think you can," he said with weighty perception. "Having worn these shoes all these years. Wrongly." His voice dropped into his chest.

Her own chest ached, unable to stand seeing such a strong man humbled.

"What happened?" She tucked her cold hands beneath her arms, still unable to believe he was even here, let alone with such a message.

"Arturo has gambling debts. Big ones. It's been a problem from his twenties, not that I or anyone saw it. If he hadn't colluded with Benito and taken my design and emptied the account, framing your father for it, he might have been killed at that time. As it was, the windfall put him back in good graces with his bookie. He burned through it, though, and fell into trouble again. That's when he started badgering you to pay your father's so-called debt."

Reeve came out of his room. His scowl of confusion at having a visitor so late deepened as Cami introduced them.

"We're not talking to you. Just take the payments and stay out of our lives," Reeve growled.

Cami hadn't told him all that had transpired in Whistler, only that Dante had refused to hire her and that the payments had been going to a fake account. He was beside himself over the whole thing. They'd stopped talking about it to keep the peace.

"Dad didn't do it," she said numbly, but stating it with her own mouth didn't make it any less surreal. She explained, and Reeve swung his attention to Dante.

"When did you find this out?"

"A few days ago." Dante rubbed his stubbled jaw. "A lot has happened very quickly, but I needed to inform you and…" He drew a heavy breath. "Express my deepest regret that your father was implicated. I will be compensating you as best I can."

He reached into his jacket pocket for a narrow envelope and set it on the battered kitchen table.

"That's a reimbursement of the amount you deposited to the Benito account. There are things to unravel in terms of the settlement your father paid before leaving Italy. It's at least three times that, and you're entitled to interest and damages. You'll see in the letter from my lawyer that this is merely a deposit as a sign of good faith. More will be forthcoming. Hire your own lawyer and have them contact ours. Legal costs will be covered on my end."

"You can't be serious!" Cami exclaimed, thinking of Dante's struggle to recoup his losses the first time. "Won't that break you? I mean financially?"

Reeve made a choking noise. "Who cares? I'd like to break his face."

"Reeve!"

Dante only looked at him as if to say, *Go ahead.*

Reeve looked tempted but shook his head. "I'm going to be a surgeon. I'm not going to shatter my hand no matter how much you deserve it."

"It wasn't him, Reeve. He's as much a victim as we are."

"He took *ten years* to look at anyone but Dad. He *fired* you without even blinking."

Cami pressed her clasped hands against her navel, thinking that wasn't all he'd done.

"I want you to come back to Sicily with me," Dante said to her. A pang of fearful hope soared through her, abruptly falling when he added, "To make a statement."

"Like hell," Reeve muttered. "We'll communicate through lawyers. Stay the hell away from both of us."

"Reeve." Her brother didn't know there was another party in this who had some rights. Someone for whom she had to get things right to the best of her ability. *How?* She felt as though she was plummeting from an airplane without a chute, unable to grasp at anything solid.

"When are you leaving?" she asked Dante.

"As soon as you're packed."

"You don't owe him a damned thing, Cam."

"I have to give notice at my job. We owe rent in four days." She dug in her purse for the tips she'd brought home, intending to put it in the jar, but Dante halted her by speaking to Reeve as he pointed at the envelope he'd brought.

"There's enough to cover your tuition for the next few years along with significantly better housing. You sleep wherever you want, but she's either coming with me, or going to a hotel. I won't have her living like this one more night."

"We've already started looking for something else," Reeve said defensively.

It was true. He'd been pushing through exams and she'd been saving up for the damage deposit. His standards for himself were considerably lower than what he wanted for Cami, but now they were together and combining resources, they could afford something slightly better.

She hadn't told him yet that they would need room

for one more. It struck her that all of her plans, once again, were being shaken apart.

"My grandmother would like to see you," Dante said. "She has never known anything about this until I had to tell her that Arturo was being arrested and why. She's extremely upset that you were hurt and would like to apologize. I want to put her mind at rest sooner than later."

"That's emotional blackmail," Reeve interjected.

"Look." Cami held up staying hands. "This is too much to take in. I can't think when I smell like spilled beer and nachos. I'm getting in the shower, then going to bed. You go to your hotel or wherever you're staying. I'll text you in the morning."

Dante was still there when she emerged fifteen minutes later. She hadn't come up with anything fresh while she'd been under the weak stream of hot water. In fact, she'd only realized how exhausted she was. How worried and ill-prepared she was for a baby. How terrified she was of Dante's reaction.

He and Reeve sat at the kitchen table, each with a cup of fresh coffee steaming before them. They had the paperwork open. The tension was so electric it crackled.

"You should have told me," Reeve said as she searched out her hairbrush.

"What?" She rarely kept anything from him so couldn't imagine—

"That you two were involved in Whistler."

Her heart took a plummet into her bare feet. She

glared at Dante. "Why on earth would you tell him that?"

"He asked."

"What made you—?" She shot a look to her brother, the budding doctor.

He glared at her, and she realized he was remembering this morning, when he had asked with concern, *Did you throw up again?* It was the second time he'd caught her, but probably the tenth time it had happened.

He looked ready to spit nails. "He wasn't accepting your transfers. I couldn't figure out why."

Lovely. Now he knew the sordid depths she'd sunk to.

"I'm entitled to a private life," she muttered, digging through her bag for moisturizer, wanting to cool her hot face.

"Cami." Reeve waited until she looked at him. "We don't need this." He flicked a finger at the papers before him. "Whatever you think you have to do, you don't. With this debt off our backs, we have options. I'll take a couple years off school if necessary. We'll figure it out. We always do."

She had never loved him so much as she did in that moment. With a lump in her throat, she nodded. "Thank you. But… I should go. For Dad."

She hadn't consciously thought that through until the words left her, but she did want their father's name properly cleared.

Reeve's mouth tightened. "I'll go, then."

She shook her head. "No, I will." She also had to think about what her child might need. *Dante's* child.

She couldn't look at him. Her hands shook as she began to pack.

CHAPTER NINE

ADRENALINE HAD KEPT Dante going until he'd seen Cami. When he finally had his eyes on her, his world shattered along with the glasses she had dropped. The cold fog he'd barely acknowledged, the one that had encased him in the last month, since finding her gown on the floor, had finally lifted—only to be replaced by a more poignant, misty one. She was every bit as beautiful as he remembered, radiating light and warmth, looking soft and natural and sweet.

Until she'd seen him.

She'd closed up like a flower, a trampled one, turning away and refusing to speak to him. He had hated Arturo, then, genuinely hated his cousin for costing him this. Her.

Much as he'd loathed watching her sling beer past midnight, he had ignored his own ale in favor of drinking in the sight of her.

Until Vito had thrust her into the forefront of his mind again, he had refused to let himself reflect on his time with her. Not consciously. He had had flashes of concern, though. Was she okay? Eating? How was her leg? Every time he received a notice of a money transfer, he wondered where she was working. Where she was living.

She had seemed to favor her leg as she spent the next several hours on her feet, looking brittle and pale. Her hair had been piled in a messy knot so her neck was a fragile stem, her face closed and intent as she worked.

She smiled at her coworkers, but any sort of humor quickly died the moment her attention was forced to turn his way. Gone was the woman who had tilted cheeky grins at him and let him see inside her when they were alone.

God, he had missed her.

Now she sat beside him, but a silence had grown between them, impenetrable and thick.

He had expected more of a fight to get her on the plane, but of course she wanted to clear her father's name. Dante was anxious to do so himself.

Speaking with Reeve had been the strangest experience. Stephen's voice had come out of a face that looked so much like the man it was uncanny. Dante's throat had been thick with apology, as he saw his old friend in Reeve's demeanor. When Reeve had asked him point-blank if anything had happened between him and Cami in Whistler, pinning him with a sharp gaze, Dante had been so surprised, his face had told the truth before he could dissemble.

He'd felt stung under Reeve's disapproval like a callow youth, aware that any attempt to claim honorable intentions at this point would be met with disdain. Suspicion even.

Cami sure as hell didn't want to rekindle things. She'd made it clear she wasn't interested even before he'd told her about Arturo. She thought they were *toxic*.

Yet here she was. Quiet and compliant beside him. Subdued almost. If not for the hint of steel in her as she'd spoken to her brother and agreed to come with him, Dante would have thought she was on the defensive. Wary. Feeling as though he held all the power again when he had definitely lost the high ground.

She was probably tired. He was. Sick and tired. From the moment Vito had told him Arturo was behind the theft, Dante had been nauseous. Absolutely gutted at the cost to Cami and her brother. Seeing how they lived had made it worse. He'd been completely sincere in saying he wouldn't let her live like that for one more night.

Along with fresh betrayal, fresh grief had hit. Stephen's loss was that much more unjust and difficult to bear. All the things Dante had seen in the man a decade ago, the belief in his ideas, the encouragement and desire for him to succeed, the fatherly pride, had been real.

He swallowed a lump, trying to feel lucky that he'd had three excellent father figures in his life, but a sense of being cheated remained.

"I won't forgive myself for cutting your father out of my life," he told Cami as the plane leveled off and the flight attendant left to bring the chamomile tea Cami had requested. "He was a good friend. I shouldn't have left his children to fend for themselves."

Cami turned from watching the lights fade at the edge of the black blanket that was the Pacific.

"I can't do this yet." Her voice was as wispy as the smoke of a snuffed flame. "I'm too tired to make sense of it. I just want to drink my tea and fall asleep and unpack all this when we get to Sicily. Do you mind?"

"No." He wanted to take her hand, console her. Say all the things that were weighing on his chest. "Use the stateroom." He nodded at the door behind them.

"Your private jet has bedrooms?" She snorted. "How many? Is there an indoor pool? A bowling alley?"

He couldn't tell if that was a dig or merely her dry wit rallying. "Just the one stateroom. And the theater." He nodded at the screen that showed their flight path.

"I'm fine here." Her elbows tucked into her waist, and she looked out the window at the void of charcoal.

He pinched the bridge of his nose.

"I wasn't presuming to join you. I won't come in unless I have to wake you because of turbulence. Then you'll have to come back to your seat."

She looked into the watery gold of her tea, but her mouth quivered. "I'm fine."

Tiny, tiny words that made his lungs fill with concrete.

She nursed her tea for the next half hour, then

watched out the window again. Eventually, she fell asleep. He unbuckled her himself and carried her into the bed, so very tempted to lie down and hold her. There was a gaping wound from the base of his throat to the pit of his belly. He needed the compress of her warmth to stem the loss.

Instead, he draped a light blanket over her and went back to his seat where he dozed fitfully and snapped awake from dreams that she had disappeared from the plane.

She must have been as exhausted as he was. When he finally did wake from a deep sleep, his neck held a dull ache and his eyes were like sandpaper. Most of their flight had gone by.

"No, I'm totally fine," Cami was saying in a low voice to the attendant. "I just don't travel well. Toast would be great. Thanks."

"Air sick?" he asked as she came to her seat.

She was pale, her hair was finger-combed and she smelled faintly of toothpaste. "It happens," she murmured, not meeting his eyes in favor of making a thorough study out the window.

"Another few hours." He pointed at the progress map, which showed them halfway over the Mediterranean.

Despite the circumstance, he was looking forward to showing her his homeland, hoping for some reason that she would love it as much as he did.

"Dante…" She wore a tortured expression as she turned her face to meet his gaze.

The gravity in her tone was so ominous his lungs

seized. His ears rang as he strained to hear her. "What's wrong?"

"I'm pregnant."

"Don't you dare ask me if it's yours," she whispered, glancing toward where the flight attendant would appear at any second.

She risked a glance at him, trembling as she had been since rising in a rush of morning sickness. She couldn't read his expression. He was a master at hiding his thoughts.

The flight attendant came to draw the table down from the wall and serve their breakfast. It was a meal of loaded silence and impossible entanglements.

When they were alone again, Cami said, "I need to know if it really was just revenge. Clearly I'm very gullible, and I know how angry you were—"

"Cami." His hand closed over her wrist, gentle, but heavy as a manacle. "I'm going to need some time."

The pressure of his touch over her pulse was so profound, her blood throbbed into his fingers like an open wound. Emotion pressed into the backs of her eyes. She couldn't swallow.

After a long minute, he released her to sip his coffee, then asked, "When did you find out?"

"A few days ago. I didn't do it on purpose."

"We." Was it her imagination, or was there a euphoric quality beneath his even, fact-finding tone? "Were you going to tell me?"

She realized she was wringing her hands and made them settle into her lap. "I hadn't worked out what to do. When you showed up last night... How are we like this? One catastrophe after another?"

He might have flinched, but the attendant brought fresh coffee.

They finished their meal in a quiet that was almost companionable, harking back to their comfortable mornings in Whistler. The ones that had given her hope they had something more than revenge and debts, blame and rancor.

"You're keeping it." She couldn't tell if that was an order or a request.

"Hopefully," she murmured. "One never knows. That's why you're not supposed to tell anyone in the first trimester."

He burned a hole through her with his gaze.

She lifted her shoulders defensively. "I've been sideswiped by life a lot. I'm not going to assume this will go as I hope it will."

He closed his eyes. "The honesty of you. I was better off when I thought it was all lies."

He didn't say he also hoped she had a successful pregnancy, and she was too unprepared to face his answer by asking if he did. They didn't talk much after that. He took several calls, speaking Sicilian, and she tried to read a book on her phone until they were preparing to land.

As her ears popped, she looked out and bonked her head into the window, trying to keep the gleaming peak in her sight. "Is that Mount Etna?"

His mouth quirked, the first softening she'd seen in him. "Yes. Why?"

Heart wobbling in thrill, she said, "I'm a mountain geek. It's so beautiful."

"I thought you only went nerd over skis."

"It's related." She leaned as far as she could, but lost sight of the peak as the plane banked. "When I first came to Italy, I spoke to a retiree who was ticking off every ski slope in Europe as a sort of bucket list thing. I didn't even know Mount Etna had a resort, but he said it was one of his favorites, that the views of the Mediterranean were spectacular. I made my own list and read up on all of the mountains, but this one seemed like such a long shot even before we had to go back to Canada."

"You can't ski," he reminded. "Not for a while."

Because she was pregnant. Taken unawares by the first big adjustment she would make in her life for the sake of the one growing inside her, she murmured a stunned "No," of agreement.

She wasn't upset by the need to take care, but the fact she once again faced a period of dark unknown distressed her. She would get through it, she knew she would, but the not knowing *how* brought a tightness to her chest. Just like that, the air grew heavy and oppressive.

Maybe it was because they were landing. She was suddenly quite homesick.

But she felt strangely at peace when she left the jet and walked across the tarmac to Dante's cobalt-blue sports car. There was something in his calm confidence that reassured her. He put the top down so the verdant afternoon air blew across her skin as he started away from the private airfield and she sighed, relaxing.

He pointed out the odd landmark as he drove, but mostly they let the breeze snap around them, blowing away travel weariness.

Cami couldn't stop craning her neck, utterly entranced. The stamp of centuries was everywhere, providing a sense of permanence and endurance.

Eventually he drove the car up a winding single lane through a vineyard, climbing to a hillock and cutting through a break in hedges to circle a fountain in front of a huge stone building. She dragged her gaze from a view that went for miles, expansive and breathtaking, and took in the worn stones of the courtyard and the vines climbing the front of what looked like a medieval castle.

"Is this a hotel?"

"It's my home." She heard the laughter in his voice and scowled at his back as he left the car.

How was she supposed to know that? She had known he was rich, but hadn't realized he was *this* rich. She was still taking that in from the passenger seat when he opened her door and offered a hand to help her out.

"It's beautiful," she murmured. *Intimidating.*

"It's a bit of a relic. My grandfather modernized with electricity and new plumbing, but aside from overhauling the kitchen a few years ago, I've only been keeping up on the necessary repairs. Noni's very comfortable. I don't like to displace her for anything that isn't absolutely necessary."

"Bernadetta's here?"

"Of course."

"But what will she think—" She realized he held her hand and carefully lifted hers away. "I don't want her to know I'm…"

It was hard, very hard, to look into his eyes, especially when his expression turned so grave. "Nothing is going to happen to it, Cami."

He couldn't *know* that.

"We're already dealing with enough. Me and her," she decided firmly. "Let's put off adding to it."

A muscle pulsed in his jaw, but he eventually said, "If you insist."

"I'm actually getting my way with you for a change?" she said as he retrieved her backpack from the trunk.

"You've had your way with me many times," he drawled.

Her breath left her in a sensual punch as she recalled teasing him while trying on dresses. He'd let her take the lead more than once in their lovemaking, but she knew there was an element of *allowing* her. Dante was always the one in control. Wasn't he?

He was certainly tightly leashed right now, all vestiges of sexual memory gone as he showed her to a guest suite. "These rooms are yours, and you should already be connected to our Wi-Fi." He held up a phone and pointed to a tablet. "Call your brother. He'll want to know you've arrived safely. Please dress for dinner at seven. Your clothes are in the wardrobe."

He left her to explore her room, and she was grateful for the time to collect herself. She left a message for Reeve, dozed in the bath, then glanced in the closet, recognizing the dresses as the ones Dante had bought for her in Whistler.

She didn't know what to make of that, but as she glanced across the vineyard from her personal balcony and took in the abundance and sheer *richness* of her surroundings, she couldn't bring herself to greet his grandmother in her worn jeans and thinning T-shirt. She found the cache of makeup she'd also left in his suite that last night and painted some confidence onto her anxious face, then wriggled herself into a dress that still had a tag on it.

When he knocked, he was freshly showered and shaved, smelling deliciously of soap and spice and something she instinctively recognized as Sicilian. It was the scent of his home. The source of all that he was. Oh, he filled her up with yearning.

He took in her simple blue dress with its sweetheart neckline and rib-hugging bodice over an A-line skirt without comment. It was the most modest in the bunch. She was trying to show some decorum in front of his grandmother, but found herself shifting her feet, aching for a sign he liked what he saw. That he still found her attractive.

That he wanted to play a silly game of modeling with her. *Foreplay.*

She blushed and looked at his polished shoes.

"This way." He waved a hand, crushing her fragile ego with his absence of response.

She made herself hold her chin high and her

shoulders back as they followed a corridor of rich red carpet. It was painful, though. She suspected the paintings were originals by men whose names were revered. She felt hideously unsophisticated that she didn't have the background to know or recognize their value.

Bernadetta rose to meet her when Cami and Dante entered the lounge.

"Oh, my dear." She looked older, which made Cami sad. The poor woman had to be devastated, first at having been kept in the dark, then on learning her grandson had not only committed crimes, but was facing the consequences.

Cami warmed the trembling hands that the old woman extended. "You have enough to worry about. Please don't be upset for me. I'm fine."

Dante made a noise, and Cami caught a flash of impatience on his face. She was stung by it, but focused on Bernadetta, sitting with her on the sofa to reassure her.

"You were so kind to me that day. You *are* so kind. And our family has treated you so terribly." Bernadetta's voice creaked.

"It's not your fault."

"Isn't it? Perhaps I was too lenient with Arturo's mother. She was my wild child. We should have brought Arturo to live with us after she divorced. He might have turned out differently." She lifted her rosary beads and pressed her lips to them.

Cami gently squeezed Bernadetta's free hand.

"Please don't dwell on things that can't be changed.

Dante and I will make it right. You don't have to worry about me. Why don't you tell me about your visit with your niece in Vancouver? Did you see everything you were hoping to?"

"*Grazij*, for taking her mind off things," Dante said a few hours later, when his Noni had gone to bed and he was alone with Cami.

"She's so sweet. But I'm insanely curious about your home theater now." She moved to the rail on the south terrace that overlooked the lower slopes. "How could I have guessed it's an ancient *amphitheater*?"

The music had started while they were finishing dinner, catching Cami's attention and prompting his grandmother to describe the site built by the Greeks and restored with great care—and expense—by his grandfather, at Noni's behest. One of her greatest pleasures was listening to the pitches by theater companies and choosing the season's starlight production.

"We could walk down if you like. It sounds like they're still rehearsing. Unless you're tired?"

"My body thinks it's the middle of the day. I'd love to." She fetched a wrap, and they started down the path. After a moment, she drew a deep breath and let it out. "It smells fantastic out here. Is that orange blossom?"

"We have a grove, yes. How is your leg?"

"I'm fine." She halted abruptly to demand, "Did you just *tsk* me?"

"You say it *all the time*. You're not fine." More than jet lag was putting the strain around her eyes, and he had noted the subtle way she was favoring one leg. Then there was the pregnancy. He was still reeling under that news.

"I'm totally fine." She hugged her wrap closer and continued walking. "You don't know me."

"Untrue," he said under his breath, but she halted again.

It was dark, turning her eyes into dark pools with a pinprick of light as she stared up at him.

"Everything you've thought about me has been a wrong impression." She turned away, saying with anguish, "Everything I thought about you was mis-interpretation."

Toxic. He kept hearing her say that, and it scored his soul every single time.

Yet, she carried his child. Wanted it.

The news of his impending fatherhood burned like a fuse, wanting to explode out of him, but who could he tell? His grandmother would love to hear it, but she would be devastated if something happened and *damn* Cami for putting that grain of doubt in his mind. He was already that attached to the idea of sharing a child with her, he would be devastated if it failed to happen.

"Dante!"

They came into the clearing of lights, and people stopped packing up water bottles and notebooks to greet him. He introduced Cami to the director and his cast. They were kind enough to move back onto the stage and perform part of a scene for her, much to her astonishment and delight.

"I'm sorry I won't see the actual performance," she

said as they were walking back up the hill toward the villa. "That was amazing."

"Why won't you?"

"They said it opens in a month. I can't imagine I'll be here more than a couple of weeks."

He snorted at her naïveté. "You'll be able to see as many performances as you like. You live here now."

She halted in the middle of the darkened vineyard and flung around to face him.

"We're getting married, Cami. You had to know that."

Maybe she had given up the fantasy of being swept off her feet long ago, but seriously? That was his proposal? All her girlhood dreams went down the toilet in a single flush.

"Be still my heart," she muttered.

"Neither of us has a choice," he added, making her want to bark out a laugh at how brutal he was being.

"You're out of your mind." She started toward the villa again, but he caught her arm.

"Stay here. The windows are open. She might wake up and hear us if we get any closer."

"Are you listening to yourself?"

"Are you? Duty to family is everything to me." His grip firmed as he impressed the words through her. "*You* are family now." He drew her forward a step and set his free hand on her stomach, splaying his fingers and drawing a deep breath, as if he was overcome by the magnitude of her pregnancy.

The world stilled, and she imagined she could feel

their baby's heartbeat rocking through both of them, hammering them together in indelible little pulses.

"Our baby might be, but I'm not." She said it to remind herself as much as him. "What are you going to do about the rest of your family? Abandon the cousin who is like a brother to you?"

Dante's breath hissed through his teeth. He dropped his hands from her, bunching them into fists. "He could have destroyed all of this." He jerked his head at their surroundings. "He abandoned me first. All of us."

"Has he confessed?"

"No."

"So things could still change. I want to believe Arturo is behind the theft. You have no idea how badly I need that to be the truth, but this nightmare never lets me wake up. And quite frankly—" she looked to the house, throat tight "—I can't help thinking you might wish my father *was* the real culprit. That way you wouldn't have to dredge this up again. If you don't already resent me for not being to blame, you soon will. Everyone in your family will."

"That's not true. My grandmother doesn't."

"This is going to drag on for years, Dante. It will be awful and expensive and draining. *I know how awful it will be.* You're going to want to point fingers. I don't want to be married to you when you decide you hate me—more than you already do."

She had to quit talking then. Her throat became too small.

"And now we come to the truth of the matter. I'm not the one filled with hate, am I?"

A ferocious ball of heat rose in her. "Okay, fine, yes. I hate you." She spat in a hiss, trying to keep her voice down. "Whether it was Arturo or Benito didn't matter. The person pressing like a heel onto my life all this time was *you*. I am brimming with resentment toward you, and I hate myself for being so weak as to sleep with you and get *pregnant*. There is no way on this earth that I want to be chained to you for a lifetime."

"Yet here we are," he bit out with a similar crack of frustration in his tone as he took her by the upper arms and pulled her close. "Bound by the child we conceived. But if you think that's all that chains us, you weren't paying attention when we made that baby." He covered her mouth with his own, kissing her with such ferocity, he burned away everything except the searing passion that had existed between them from the moment they'd met.

It was exactly as it had been so many times between them, running quickly beyond their control. She twined her arms around his neck and dug her fingers into his hair, pressing him down to deepen the pressure of the kiss, opening her mouth wide beneath his and meeting his tongue with her own.

It was struggle and reunion. Anger and anguish. Clash and fury and a clawing desperate heartache that made her pull at him, rather than push him away.

His natural need to dominate had him trying to take control, but she wouldn't have it. Not this time.

She was too furious. He had used her, and this time she used him. She scraped his bottom lip with her teeth and arched herself to wriggle against him.

Excitement expanded his chest in a hissing breath. He skimmed the dress from her shoulders in one abrupt move that had her pulling back, eyes widening with shock as the air touched her naked torso. They were outside, in the vineyard.

"You're right," he growled. "Not here."

As he seemed to grapple himself back under control, something defiant and angry and incredibly hurt moved in her. She needed his passion to heal it. She needed to know she was stronger than him in this moment. That her will could prevail. She needed him to be as overcome as she was.

He started to turn her toward the house, and she flung herself into him.

"Yes, here." She leaped, opening her legs and forcing him to catch her with a grunt, then twined her legs around his waist.

They kissed again, but he swore against her lips as he took her to the ground beneath him. Cool grass tickled her shoulder blades and her sandal fell off.

His hot mouth slid down her neck, and she opened her eyes to the stars. "I can't bear how easily you do this to me, Dante. Even when I win, you win. You own me."

He set his forehead against her jawbone. "It's the same for me, damn you. How do you not know that? You're all I can see right now. All that exists in my world. Do you think I'm proud of this reaction?"

The weight of his hips sat heavily between her thighs, pressing his hardness where she was aching with anticipation. That, coupled with his words, were all she needed to sink back into the throes. Her thighs shifted to better hug him, and her fingers began pulling at the top button on his shirt.

Even as she warned herself to cling to some sense, Dante was dipping his head to steal a taste of her nipple. Every other thought died then, lost beyond how good he made her feel.

She knew she ought to feel used by him. Manipulated even. But the care he took, and the way he seemed to shudder with restraint as he tasted her with such a sense of worship, was badly needed reassurance of his desire for her. Of this mad connection that shouldn't exist, but did.

She pressed his shoulder so she could get at the rest of his buttons, then didn't bother with opening them. She pulled his shirt apart so the buttons gave way until finally the heat of his chest settled over hers. They both groaned. His mouth climbed and paused as it often did on her collarbone, where the tiny raised white line always seemed to need a lick of his attention. Then his teeth scraped her nape and finally he kissed her again.

A moment later, he dispatched her panties into the weeds. She lay beneath him in the soil while he lifted on an elbow enough to open his pants. She guided him with her own hand, taking his damp crest into her core with a sob of relief.

He entered with a fierce thrust and a carnal groan.

They were barely human in that moment. All civilization gone as they mated.

She scraped her hands down his back beneath his shirt, encouraging his hard thrusts as she raced toward the crisis. Her climax was so quick and shattering, she cried out with loss. He smothered her muted scream with his mouth and didn't stop moving. The rhythms of his thrusts kept her in that glittering plane of orgasm, not allowing her to descend. Within moments, she was overcome and sobbing out her ecstasy again, but still he didn't relent.

Over and over the waves of pleasure ground through her, until she was unable to tell where she ended and he began. All she knew was that he was the instrument of her ecstasy and she would never let him go.

Only then, as she accepted that he was a part of her, did she feel the muscles of his back tighten. He lifted his head and tilted it back, howling at the sky as he finally joined her in supreme joy.

She was softness and light, her hair silken against his nose, her scent clean and familiar and now carrying the aromas of his home. Latent orange blossoms and fertile volcanic ash.

The civilized man in him wanted to apologize for having her in the dirt like this, but there was no room in him for groveling. Possessiveness engulfed him. She was his. If he had to prove it again, he would. Every remaining hour of their lives, if necessary.

He couldn't drink in enough of her. Her throat, her

still racing pulse beneath his lips, her sweet cry of surrender still ringing in his ears. The warm round-ness of her perspiration-dampened breast hot in his palm.

As afterglow went, this was more like survival of a shipwreck. They were washed ashore, lucky to be alive.

"I didn't use a condom." He hadn't even thought of it.

"The damage has been done."

True, but he still should have at least thought about it. Conscious decision-making had abandoned him, however.

"Here I was afraid that you didn't want me any-more. Or wouldn't," she murmured.

"I don't see this wearing off."

"But it doesn't solve anything, Dante." She pressed his shoulder, urging him to gently extricate and roll away, allowing her to sit up. "It changes nothing."

Bits of grass stuck to her ivory skin. He brushed at her back and shoulders. She was like a goddess in the moonlight, casting a spell with her iridescent beauty. Her narrow spine broke something inside him that had hardened over the years and threat-ened to solidify again, every time he thought of his cousin's betrayal.

"In fact, if anything proves how disastrous our marriage would be, this is it. We're each other's downfall."

"Did you feel belittled by our affair?" He feared it was too late to ask that, having taken her on the hard-packed soil of the vineyard. "Because it was always just this for me. Madness, yes. A compulsion, but not something I was using to hurt you."

He heard her swallow, then she said, "I feel small. Made to feel small, because your feelings weren't involved."

"Were *yours*?"

Cami couldn't bear how vulnerable that question made her feel. She was peeled right down to the core by their lovemaking and had to dig deep for a deflection. "I was a virgin. Of course I built it into something bigger than it was."

"It was big, Cami. It meant something to me, too."

She couldn't look at him for fear he would somehow trick her into giving up her autonomy all over again. "That doesn't mean we should continue doing this. Or make it worse by getting married."

"'Worse?' What kind of a husband do you think I would be?"

"You don't want to marry anyone," she reminded him. "Certainly not me."

"That was true when I said it." His hot hand returned to splay across her lower back. "But I want to be married to the mother of my child. Maybe I didn't see myself marrying you when we were having our affair, but I've since seen enough passion, and enough compatibility in other areas, that I think we could build something."

"You said this was a compulsion. I don't want to be your drug addiction."

"You called us toxic. Let's both find a kinder vocabulary."

He sounded short, and she felt as though she hovered on a tightrope, carefully inching along into an abyss, in danger of falling at any moment, not even able to look up to the other side for fear it wasn't even there.

"You've been living in squalor, Cami." He sat up beside her, and his profile was jagged shadows and brutal angles. "I can't expect you to forgive me for that. Marriage is the best compensation I can offer. You'll be entitled to half my wealth, and our child inherits all of it."

"I don't want your money, Dante." She sighed with a pang.

"What do you want? To live alone in Canada, denying me access to my child and denying our child all of this? You're right. I won't let you have that."

She wanted his *heart*, but she never got what she wanted anyway. She threaded her arms into her dress and found her feet. "Can we just get through the investigation and figure out the next steps after that?"

He hitched his pants into place as he stood, then brushed his knees and looked to button his shirt before shaking his head at finding all of them gone.

"The effect you have on me," he muttered. "If you need time to get used to the idea, fine."

She snorted and walked away.

After breakfast the next morning, Bernadetta showed Cami around the gallery of family photos with great pride, offering up dozens of names and relationships. Cami would never remember all of them, but she was particularly taken by Bernadette's wedding photo. The young Bernadetta looked overwhelmed, but her husband was so handsome and powerful looking, Cami knew exactly how she'd been drawn into marrying him.

"Dante really takes after him. You must have loved him very much."

Bernadetta hesitated, which made Cami snap a startled look at her.

"Oh, I did. Very deeply." Bernadetta smiled at Cami's reaction, then a wistfulness passed over her expression as she looked back at the photo. "But it took some time. Ours was a marriage of convenience. It was a work-around for some red tape he was trying to avoid. I wanted out from under my father's thumb—he was a lovely man, but very strict. I somehow thought I'd have better chances with Leo. Dante takes after him in temperament, too."

"Oh. Poor you," she teased.

"Yes. They're a dominant force, the Gallo men." She looked at Cami as though she could see right through her. "And they don't love easily, but when they do give their heart, it is forever."

Cami was trying really hard not to wish for something so impossible. Nevertheless, yearning colored her voice when she asked, "What about you? Did it take a long time?"

"I resisted as long as I could. I wasn't even planning to sleep with him, expecting to save myself for my 'real' husband. That didn't last a day." Bernadetta gave her a wink. "He was very persuasive."

Cami couldn't help laughing. It was too astonishing for this old woman to be making jokes about sex.

"If I hadn't had a stubborn streak of my own, those first years might have been easier, but I needed some backbone to stand up to him. We found our way, though. So will you and Dante."

Cami's pulse skipped. Her first thought was that somehow Bernadetta had heard them in the vineyard last night, which was deathly mortifying.

"You didn't drink any of our excellent wine last night," the old woman said, her gaze sliding from her young husband to offer a soft look up at Cami. "If you think photos of you with Dante at the Tabor gala failed to catch my attention, you underestimate my desire to follow the antics of my very active family. My boys may have a few secrets from me, but I don't make it easy for them to keep them."

"I…" Cami's voice dwindled to a congestion she had to clear from her throat. "I don't want you to think I planned any of this." She *liked* Bernadetta. A lot. She didn't know how she would handle it if what seemed like her only ally turned her back on her. "It's… I'm still in shock." She wrung her hands.

"Oh, my dear, no one takes advantage of Dante. The only reason Arturo was able to was because he was that close to him all his life." Grief washed over her face as she mentioned her other grandson. "In fact, I fear Dante could be destroyed by what has occurred between them. The only thing that could save him is your forgiveness."

"Please don't put that on me, Bernadetta."

"If you reject him, if you deny him a place in his child's life, he will blame himself and sink into even more cynicism than he already possesses. I understand these last years better now, that it was more than Leo's passing and Dante's having to take up the mantle that made him so hard. But that's also how I know he's in danger of letting bitterness destroy him. It could close him off to me and everyone else who cares about him. The only thing that could counter that is love."

"No pressure," Cami muttered, tucking her hair off her face with a slide of her finger. "He doesn't love me." It was so painful, it came out as a whisper.

"Not yet, but there is only one way to keep a man that strong, strong. By giving him a weakness who is equally strong. I'm speaking from experience."

"I'm not you, Bernadetta."

"No, you're far braver than I ever was. Do you think I tried to break land speed records down an icy slope? Pshhh."

"Here you are," Dante said, coming into the lounge. "We should leave soon." He was taking her to the first meeting with investigators today.

Bernadetta grasped Cami's hand and beamed a smile at him. "You've made me the happiest woman, Dante. I don't know how I could get through all that we face without something as wonderful as a wedding and grandchildren to look forward to."

Cami choked.

Dante shot her a look, but it was the flinty one he'd sent her when Bernadetta offered to send them skiing. *Let her have this.*

He leaned to kiss his grandmother's cheek, saying, "I'm glad you're pleased."

"She guessed and I didn't know what to say," Cami grumbled when they were in the car a few minutes later. "I'm sorry."

"Why?" he said dryly. "Now we can sleep together."

"You—" She rolled her eyes. "You're really not angry?"

"I told you last night I wanted to marry you. You came around a lot sooner than I expected. *Grazij*, Noni."

"I still think it's a terrible idea."

And yet, as the days passed, he made it easy for her to think otherwise. Despite how difficult their meetings were, or how short his temper became in some of them, he was extremely protective and solicitous toward her. Between the appointments, he showed her his island home, spoiled her with impulsive purchases and pestered her to eat properly and mind her leg and wear sunscreen. They were back to their camaraderie in Whistler, but without the clock ticking down. It was poignantly sweet, building up her hopes.

At night—oh, the nights. Could she spend the rest of her life joining her naked body to his every single night? There, at least, she had no doubts.

In fact, as the days wore into high summer, and

her new doctor confirmed her pregnancy was coming along with textbook perfection, and her brother's flight was booked so he could give her away at her wedding, she almost began to believe they had a chance.

She almost believed that someday, somehow, Dante might come to love her as she had come to love him.

Was she fooling herself all over again? Doubts crept in when she was alone like this, flicking through wedding dress images on the terrace. She lifted her gaze from the tablet to the idyllic view toward Mount Etna, astonished to find herself in the middle of a fairy tale.

She had learned the hard way not to believe in them, so how was she here, living one? How long could it really last?

Desperate for reassurance, she went looking for her intended. He had a lot of pressures on him right now, but no matter how busy he was with work or anything else, he always looked pleased to see her. Sometimes he took a break for coffee with her, occasionally a flirty kiss turned into a sexy tussle on top of his desk. If nothing else, his physical infatuation with her kept her heartened for their future.

Today, however, he had someone with him. She paused beyond the cracked door, not wanting to interrupt, then freezing to the floor when she heard her name.

If one of his more passionate relatives had confronted him, Dante might have taken it less seriously, but his uncle Giorgio was a tax auditor, one of the steadiest, most analytical and logical men Dante knew. He was also a neutral party, being married to Noni's fourth daughter and never having shown favorites among his many nieces and nephews. He'd always been the ultimate egalitarian mediator, in fact.

"Arturo's behavior aside, her pregnancy is awfully convenient."

"You're a bit late for 'the talk,' *zu*."

"Have you had a paternity test? This wedding is very rushed. It's not like you to be so impulsive, Dante."

He was aware. When he had gone to Canada, he'd been driven by a need to provide restitution for Arturo's crime against Cami and her family. Yes, he could admit that deep down he had longed to see her again, but given the circumstances, he hadn't expected her to get on a plane with him, let alone into his bed. Her pregnancy had been a convenience for *him*, allowing him to pull her back into the intimate relationship he wanted.

Needed.

Damn, that scared him.

"You don't even know for certain that the baby is yours. We already have a lot to lose. Insist on a paternity test before you marry her and wait until Arturo's guilt is proved in court. You aren't responsible for his actions or anyone else's, but you are responsible for your own. Do your due diligence. Be certain this time that you're not just seeing what you want to see."

That stung because it was true. He had never once suspected Arturo's involvement because it was too great a betrayal to consider. He had let himself see Stephen as the thief instead.

"Keep your eyes open," Giorgio continued. "Even if the baby is yours, you have to question her motives. She was in a tight spot with you. It's not as if this is a love child."

Dante burned under that remark, trying to shutter himself to such a possibility because the idea of being in love meant being even more vulnerable to her than he already was.

"Point taken," he acknowledged, only wanting his uncle to leave before he betrayed himself further. "I'll give it more thought."

Once he was gone, Dante stood at the window, only realizing as her lounger stayed empty that he was waiting to see Cami come back to it. He was entirely too susceptible to her. Too dependent.

But the piece of the puzzle that his uncle didn't have, Dante realized, was that Cami had never lied to him. He had begun their association with condemnation of her and her family, yet she had proved herself again and again as truthful and trustworthy.

Sweat popped onto his brow as a disturbingly vivid memory came over him of that first time she'd proved it. *Her* first time. She had trusted him with herself. Then, when she had had a chance to walk away from him with perhaps not riches, but certainly a bonanza by the standards she'd been forced to live under, she had left it on the floor of his hotel suite.

She had tried to pay her father's debt in good faith and, even more shocking, when she had learned her father was innocent, she hadn't taken a stake to Dante's heart. She hadn't hidden his child from him. She had agreed to marry him, despite all the ways he'd damaged her life.

At no time had she betrayed him. She was the most steadfast, loyal, *lovable*—

A flash of blue caught his eye. His chauffeur was carrying her battered, *full* backpack to the car.

Oh, hell, no.

What could she possibly say to Bernadetta except, *I'm sorry*?

Hovering the pen over the paper, Cami almost wrote, *I'm not brave like you*, but that just made her feel ashamed of herself for running away. What was she supposed to do, though? Put up with having an ax over her head forever? She couldn't. If today wasn't the end, then something else would come up.

Something *always* happened. She would far rather be the one to choose how she and Dante parted than invest more of herself and feel the break that much more deeply in the future. It already hurt so badly she could hardly breathe.

"What the hell do you think you're doing?" Dante asked, coming into the library and shutting the door with a firmness that was very close to a slam.

The sharp noise cut into her, making the agony she had been holding off flood through her in a wave. She tried sitting straighter in his grandfather's antique rolling chair, but when Dante came to lean on the desk and glare at her over it, she wanted to wither. She pushed to her feet, chest tight.

"My Sicilian isn't great," she told him, hearing the strain in her voice "But I got the gist. You want a paternity test. Fine." She threw down the pen. "But I'm not going to marry a man who won't take my word on something so basic."

"You're going to let one ugly accusation destroy the life we're trying to make? Which one of us is having trouble trusting?"

"Oh, come on, Dante. One accusation is all it took the first time. My entire *life* is still being destroyed by one ugly accusation."

Through the moisture gathering in her eyes, she saw his head snap back as though he took her words as a blow on the chin. His face contorted with emotion. Something that might have been despair shadowed his eyes.

"And you can't forgive me for believing my cousin instead of your father."

How was it that she could withstand her own pain, but not his?

"It's not about forgiveness. I wanted to believe my father was innocent despite the evidence." She tapped her chest. "I completely understand why you didn't imagine your cousin could have done it. We want to believe in the people we love."

"That tells me how *you* feel, then, doesn't it?" His face was sharp and tight, his lips white.

How could she admit to her own love when, "*You* don't love *me*!"

That was the excruciating heartbreak she was trying to escape, unable to face it when her own heart was so completely his.

"You will never believe in me, despite how much I've tried to prove…" She had to bite her lips to steady them. Swallowed past the tightness in her throat. "I can't live my life like that. If you don't trust me, I can't trust this." She waved between them. "I won't build castles on clouds." She started to walk around the desk and out of the room.

"I love you," he ground out.

The words went into her as an arrow, making her suck in a deep breath. "Don't. At least keep truth between us."

"You dare to suggest I would lie about *that*?" He grasped her by the shoulders, swinging her to face him. "I should have—" His hands tightened briefly on her, revealing the deep emotions gripping him. "I should have said it when we were still in Whistler, but do you think I knew what it was when I've never felt *this* kind of love before? Passionate and intense and so quick to rip me apart I still can't take it in?"

"Dante." She pleaded for him not to make this harder. "I don't get happily-ever-after. My life never works out. It always falls apart, and I can't bear that I'll start to believe the things you're saying only to have it all disappear. I have to go now, before it's more than I can survive."

"It's already too late. Leaving would kill us both."

She teared up and he smoothed his hand over her

hair, soothing her as he drew her stiff body into his chest and pressed his mouth to her temple.

"This is my fault. I've destroyed your ability to believe in the future, but you have to give me a chance to fix that. To prove we have one."

"We're always going to be who we are." She set her hands on his waist, not sure if she wanted to embrace him or push him away. "The past is always going to have the power to rear up and destroy us. I can't live like that, waiting for it to happen. I can't build something that means everything to me, then lose it."

"So you want to throw it away now? No. Listen to me." His arms tightened and his breath stirred the hair near her ear, sending tingles down her nape. "We *are* who we are, but not who you think. We aren't enemies. We were meant for one another, Cami. If you leave today, we'll only come back together later. It's inevitable. Your father invited me to come see you ski, did you know that?" He drew back to look her in the eye. "I made an excuse, but if things hadn't gone to hell, I would have come one day and watched you and fallen for you then, because you're that amazing and wonderful."

"I was fourteen," she scoffed, closing her eyes against the alternate reality where she crushed on the young man who so impressed her father and he loved her back. She won medals while he designed futuristic cars. They married and had children who grew up knowing their grandparents.

"I would have waited for you. I did wait." He growled. "You didn't find anyone else, either. It took far too long, but we came together again under yes, difficult circumstances, but we *came together*. What are the chances of that? Hmm? And that we would fall for each other even with this mess between us?"

He combed her hair back from her face, tilting up her chin and letting his gaze wander the delicate line of her jaw, grazing gentle fingertips against her cheek and the sensitive hollow beneath her ear.

"We scare the hell out of each other, our feelings are so strong. So yes, our trust needs time to grow deeper roots. It's been rocky, but even if you aren't ready to believe in me, you have to believe in *us*."

Her chin crinkled. She searched his eyes for some evidence he was being fanciful, but he wasn't a man to make up nonsense.

"Can you really look past…everything?"

"I already did, when I kissed you the first time in Whistler. Can you?"

"I want to."

The tension in his hand, where it had slid to the side of her neck, eased into a gentle caress. "Because you love me?"

She could hardly take in that he was using that word. With her. Her chest felt too full, like it would split from the pressure swelling her heart. "I do," she admitted with a scrape in her throat. "I love you a lot."

He grew very somber. "You humble me with your capacity to forgive. Your generous heart. I will never take you for granted. You *can* believe in me. I *will* prove it to you."

He started to kiss her, but her hand went to the

middle of his chest, holding him off. "But what about the paternity test?"

His expression softened. "Of course you're carrying my baby," he chided. "I could hardly tell my uncle I remember exactly when we conceived, in vivid detail, could I? My only regret is that you were angry with me that day. Unsure of us. But we were already in love, Cami. Damn right that's my child you're carrying."

He placed his hand over the very slight bump that was really only visible to him because he knew her shape so well. She blushed, but teared up, too.

"It was a very small chance we took that day, yet look how it's binding us together," he said, lifting his gaze to hers.

Perhaps they *were* fated.

As the light in his eyes continued to pour through her, she began to believe it. With a shaky smile, she lifted onto tiptoes and let the love on his lips absorb into her soul. She didn't imagine she could taste it. She knew it as a tangible thing that filled her with growing joy and a euphoric certainty that was so sweet and precious, her tears sprinkled past her lashes onto her cheeks.

Three weeks later, she took her brother's arm. He was terrifically handsome in a morning suit. Her dress had an empire waist to hide her small bump.

"I don't want to give you away," Reeve said with a rueful smile. "You're all I have. But you look so happy…"

"I am, Reeve. I really am," she said, still stunned

by it herself. The fragile trust between her and Dante had been growing exponentially, concentrating into something that centered both of them on a foundation that brought her peace for the first time in her adult life.

She spoke her vows a short time later, basking in the light of her husband's gaze. She looked to their future without trepidation and told him as much in their candlelit honeymoon suite.

"I don't know what our life will look like in ten years, but I can't wait to find out." He drew her into his arms.

Their kiss began sweet and unhurried, so tender she grew choked with emotion. He was every bit as thorough as he usually was, ringing pleasure through her again and again, but with a new quality to each touch, each kiss, each caress.

It was commitment and worship and love. So much love.

EPILOGUE

Some might call it spoiling, but Dante held their son until he fell asleep.

Leo was tall for two, all arms and legs as he dangled against Dante's shoulder. His chubby limbs dropped to the mattress as Dante gently put the boy into his toddler bed.

Cami hadn't said a thing as her husband had spent the evening doting on their son, bathing him and getting him into his pj's, then reading and finally holding him and rubbing his back until the boy's head had been heavy on his shoulder.

Leo wasn't upset or ill. No, Dante was the one who had had a very difficult day. Arturo had been sentenced and taken to prison.

When Dante had come home drained and withdrawn, seeking comfort by coddling their son, Cami had done her best not to intrude. She knew how healing a child's love was, so innocent and unconditional and pure. Anytime her own ghosts reared their head, she looked at her son and fell in love with her husband all over again for giving her their child.

Children.

This entire week had been busy and difficult, so she had kept the news to herself. They weren't consciously trying for another one, and she wasn't entirely sure how he would react. With his mind in turmoil along with his heart, she hadn't wanted to put something else on him. Maybe it was even a bit selfish of her. She didn't want something that brought her so much joy to be linked in his mind with something that was nothing but pain.

He turned and saw her watching him from the doorway to Leo's room. He checked briefly, then hitched his shoulder in a rueful shrug.

She smiled her understanding. It was the sort of telepathic communication that came between parents who didn't dare risk waking an infant by speaking aloud.

As he carried the baby monitor from their son's room and closed the door, he caught her hand and drew her toward their own room.

Her heart took the skip and jump it always did when he touched her. A warmer, more tender emotion flowed through her. It was her turn. He needed *her* now.

They didn't speak when they entered their room. He only closed the door and drew her into his arms. The baby monitor clattered onto the dresser top so he could use both hands to remove her clothing.

His urgency sent a surge of need through her. She needed this, too, she realized as their mouths met in a clashing kiss. She hadn't felt threatened by these latest events exactly, but it had been a test, taking up Dante's time and attention. She needed this conflagration to fuse them back together again.

It was frantic and quick against the wall. He exploded with a muffled cry at the same time that she did, which wasn't like him.

As he stood panting and damp against her, he said, "That was a lot more intense than I meant it to be."

With a lurch that seemed almost drunken, he straightened, pulling her with him so she clung with her thighs to his waist, keeping them joined as he took them to the bed.

"I don't mind," she told him, kissing his jaw and neck. "I like knowing you can't resist me. That I can still undermine your control."

"But you're pregnant. I should be more careful." He lowered her to the bed and came down on top of her, hardening afresh within her.

"You know?"

He frowned. "You think I don't know your body as well as you do?"

"I wasn't sure how you'd feel," she admitted, revealing the tiny wrinkle of doubt on her heart. "If you were ready for another."

"Past ready. Elated. Aren't you? Is that why you haven't said anything?"

"I'm thrilled, but I was worried it was, I don't know, more than you wanted to hear when you were dealing with so much this week."

"Are you kidding? Having good news was the only thing that kept me going. If anything, I needed to know that you and I were stronger than ever." He cupped her head in two hands, touching his lips to hers. "I needed to know you were tied even more tightly to me, so you wouldn't let the past cause you to give up on us."

"I would *never* do that," she vowed.

He smiled. "No, you won't. And neither will I. I love you."

"I love you, too. Now let's have a do-over. See if you can last a little longer this time."

"I will take that challenge, *bedduzza*," he chuckled, then set about proving his staying power.

* * * * *

If you enjoyed
CONSEQUENCE OF HIS REVENGE
by Dani Collins,
why not explore these other
ONE NIGHT WITH CONSEQUENCES *stories?*

CONTRACTED FOR THE PETRAKIS HEIR
by Annie West
A BABY TO BIND HIS BRIDE
by Caitlin Crews
A NIGHT OF ROYAL CONSEQUENCES
by Susan Stephens

Available now!

#3617 KOSTAS'S CONVENIENT BRIDE
by Lucy Monroe

Kayla's boss Andreas must marry! After she experienced the incandescent pleasure of his touch, his proposal is everything she's dreamed of. But dare she risk her heart to become a convenient wife?

#3618 THE VIRGIN'S DEBT TO PAY
by Abby Green

Merciless Luc will hold Nessa captive until her brother's debt is settled. And when undeniable attraction overwhelms them both, Nessa's innocence is the real price to pay!

#3619 CLAIMING HIS HIDDEN HEIR
Secret Heirs of Billionaires
by Carol Marinelli

Seduced then dismissed by her demanding boss Luka, Cecelia's hiding a secret—their daughter! But when Luka uncovers her deceit, there's no escaping the consequences of her passionate surrender...

#3620 THE INNOCENT'S ONE-NIGHT CONFESSION
by Sara Craven

Zandor awakened Alanna to an unknown sensuality—but shocked at her own passionate response, she fled! When Zandor reappears, this time she can't run from the sizzling intensity of their connection...

#3621 DESERT PRINCE'S STOLEN BRIDE
Conveniently Wed!
by Kate Hewitt

To reclaim his country, Zayed *must* wed. He steals away his intended...only to realize shy Olivia is the wrong woman! But with such heated chemistry between them, do they want to correct their mistake?

#3622 HIRED TO WEAR THE SHEIKH'S RING
by Rachael Thomas

As Jafar's temporary wife, Tiffany is perfect. Yet this convenient arrangement for his crown leads to passion! Is their craving enough to make Tiffany more than just the sheikh's hired bride?

#3623 SURRENDER TO THE RUTHLESS BILLIONAIRE
by Louise Fuller

Luis is shocked to learn the beautiful stranger he spent one scorching night with has also been hired by his family! He whisks Cristina away to uncover her ulterior motive...and rekindles their incendiary desire!

#3624 PRINCESS'S PREGNANCY SECRET
One Night With Consequences
by Natalie Anderson

Damon can't resist a sensual encounter with a captivating guest at a royal masquerade. But he's shocked to discover she was actually Princess Eleni—and now she's carrying his baby!

Get 2 Free Books,
Plus 2 Free Gifts—
just for trying the Reader Service!

◆HARLEQUIN *Presents*

HP17R3

"We were so hot, Cecelia, and we could have been
good, but you chose to walk away. You left. And then
you denied me the knowledge of my child and I hate you
for that." And then, when she'd already gotten the dark
message, he gave it a second coat and painted it black. "I
absolutely hate you."

"No mixed messages, then?" She somehow managed
a quip but there was nothing that could lighten this
moment.

"Not one. Let me make things very clear. I am not
taking you to Greece to get to know you better or to see
if there is any chance for us, because there isn't. I want

no further part of you. The fact is, you are my daughter's mother and she is too young to be apart from you. That won't be the case in the near future."

"How near?"

Fear licked the sides of her heart.

"I don't know." He shrugged. "I know nothing about babies, save what I have found out today. But I learn fast," he said, "and I will employ only the best, so very soon, during my access times, Pandora and I will do just fine without you."

"Luka, please…" She could not stand the thought of being away from Pandora and she was spinning at the thought of taking her daughter to Greece, but Luka was done.

"I'm going, Cecelia," Luka said. "I have nothing left to say to you."

That wasn't quite true, for he had one question.

"Did you know you were pregnant when you left?" Luka asked.

"I had an idea…"

"The truth, Cecelia."

And she ached now for the days when he had been less on guard and had called her Cece, even though it had grated so much at the time.

And now it was time to be honest and admit she had known she was pregnant when she had left. "Yes."

Don't miss
CLAIMING HIS HIDDEN HEIR
available May 2018 wherever
Harlequin Presents® books and ebooks are sold.

www.Harlequin.com

HARLEQUIN

Presents

Coming next month—Lucy Monroe's latest Harlequin Presents story!

In *Kostas's Convenient Bride*, Kayla's boss needs to marry. Can she step out of the shadows and down the aisle?

Discovering that her boss, billionaire tycoon Andreas Kostas, must marry is devastating for Kayla. Then Andreas proposes that *Kayla* wear his ring! Having experienced the incandescent pleasure of his touch, she's hidden her yearning for him ever since. It's the proposal Kayla's always dreamed of, but does she dare risk her body and her heart to become a convenient wife?

Kostas's Convenient Bride

Available May 2018